THE INCREDIBLE DIARY OF...

A Journey Into Imagination

Edited By Wendy Laws

First published in Great Britain in 2023 by:

Young Writers
Remus House
Coltsfoot Drive
Peterborough
PE2 9BF
Telephone: 01733 890066
Website: www.youngwriters.co.uk

Printed and bound in the UK by BookPrintingUK
Website: www.bookprintinguk.com
YB0560R

Foreword

Dear Diary,

You will never guess what I did today! Shall I tell you? Some primary school pupils wrote some diary entries and I got to read them, and they were EXCELLENT!

Here at Young Writers we created some bright and funky worksheets along with fun and fabulous (and free) resources to help spark ideas and get inspiration flowing. And it clearly worked because WOW!! I can't believe the adventures I've been reading about. Real people, make-believe people, dogs and unicorns, even objects like pencils all feature and these diaries all have one thing in common – they are JAM-PACKED with imagination!

Here at Young Writers we want to pass our love of the written word onto the next generation and what better way to do that than to celebrate their writing by publishing it in a book! It sets their work free from homework books and notepads and puts it where it deserves to be – OUT IN THE WORLD!

Each awesome author in this book should be SUPER PROUD of themselves, and now they've got proof of their imagination, their ideas and their creativity in black and white, to look back on in years to come!

Contents

Redfield Educate Together Primary Academy, Redfield

Diego Catavello Ron (8)	59
Sanaa Mohamed (8)	60
Eve Bridgewater (7)	62
Elliot Colebrook (8)	64
Elise Reeves (8)	65

Ruskin Academy, Wellingborough

Linda Platore (9)	66
Michaela Ward (9)	67
Theo White (8)	68
Cleopatra Leon (9)	69

St Ives Junior School, St Ives

Neve Burton (10)	70
Lacey Bolton (10)	72
Staci Vine (10)	74
Pheobe Trevorrow (10)	76
Harriet Hooper (10)	78
Keavy Devenny (10)	79
Kit McAvay (10)	80
Millie Murt (10)	81

St Mary Queen Of Martyrs RC Primary School, Hull

Abigail Macpherson (9)	82
Lilly Kate Harrison (9)	83
Ava Sutherby (9)	84
Samuel Oakes (9)	85
Reece Wright (9)	86
Sonny Runkee (9)	87
Olly Thompson (9)	88
Ava Boyton (9)	89
Benjamin Prajsnar (9)	90
Edward Macpherson (9)	91
Jacob Smalley (9)	92
Mercy-Rae Robinson (9)	93
Kaiden Howard (9)	94

St Richard's RC Primary School, Atherton

Eric Udo-Uzoagba (10)	95
Erica Udo-Uzoagba (10)	96
Abisola Ilupeju (10)	98
Alex Malaj (10)	100
Lily King (10)	102
Serena Price (10)	104
Abigail Ip (10)	106
Mia-Jayed Richards (10)	108
Lucie Sumner (10)	109
Ruby Cunliffe (9)	110
Freddie (10)	111

St Thomas The Martyr CE Primary School & Nursery, Up Holland

Nathan Chow (10)	112
Emily Dean (11)	113

Stillness Junior School, London

Ellie Plumpton (10)	114
Kitty Chambers (10)	116
Ryan Tin (10)	118
Kyla Lennon (10)	120
Rowena Streatfeild (9)	122
Isobel Minns (10)	124
Gregor Jackman (10)	126
Beatrice Roebuck (9)	128

The Stoke Poges School, Stoke Poges

Reet Gandhi (9)	129
Alice Weaver (9)	130
Gabriel Carmo (9)	132
Madeleine Briggs (9)	134
Kairon Arya (9)	136
Josephine Donnelly (9)	137
Zara Dar (9)	138
Lucy Chapman (9)	139
Anika Mandokhot (9)	140
Mia Lee (9)	141

Amellie Barrett-Allchin (9)	142
Khadija Ali (8)	143
Veer Benawra (9)	144
Hafsah Malik (9)	145
Finn McGarvey (8)	146

Yarlet School, Yarlet

Elliot Shelley (10)	147
Bertie Shammas (10)	148
Harry Cookson-Jones (11)	150
Cora Norris (11)	152
Logan Kerr (11)	153
Monty Priest (10)	154
Alexander McClean (10)	155
Dillan Siddiqi (11)	156
Harriet Moffatt (10) & Annabel	157
Emma Wells (10)	158
Megan McNulty (11)	159
Harrison Josephs (10)	160
Arthur Ratcliffe (9)	161
Martha Aitken (11)	162
Anvay Malhotra (10)	163

The Diaries

The Diary Of Natasha

Dear Diary,
My name is Natasha. My hobbies are Morris dancing, also I love geocaching. So today after school, I went over to one of the points and had a little look for it, however, when my back was turned a man sneaked up on me and kidnapped me. I screamed and screamed but no one heard me because nobody was around. I was getting very scared, sad and anxious because I didn't know what to do. However, after only a few minutes I could see light coming from the two back doors of the van so I pushed them open and jumped out and ran for my life until I got home and told my mum everything whilst gasping for air. She immediately rang the police and a few hours later we heard on the news that the man had been jailed.
Let's hope tomorrow is better.

Scarlett Rudd (10)
Coppull Primary School And Children's Centre, Coppull

The Diary OF A Dancer

Dear Diary,

Today is the day! I am going to find out whether I am accepted into the Royal Ballet of London. Every hour spent practising, every lesson, every mistake I've corrected and all the sweat, effort and even tears have come down to this moment.

I barely get to spend any quality time with my family and friends. Although all these years of training have been tough, I have loved every second of it and I really do have the most fabulous ballet teacher. She has helped me with so much, not just ballet but confidence, bravery and perseverance to continue aiming for my goal. I'm so nervous I couldn't eat breakfast this morning, but I'm still extremely excited.

The only thing I am going to struggle with is moving away from my family. Unfortunately, my parents are not able to move to London but they really want me to do this. We've already arranged to FaceTime every day and visit each other every holiday.

It's going to be very tough for me if I get accepted but this is what I have always wanted to do. I want to be on stage, I want to show the world I can dance and most importantly, do what I do best - ballet.

2

Even if I don't get in, I will still be proud of everything I have achieved over the years. I bet you already know, I'm dancing right now! Haha. I can't wait to keep you updated with my results! Please Mr Postman, hurry up!

Eowyn Gore (10)
Coppull Primary School And Children's Centre, Coppull

The Diary Of Mckenzie

Dear Diary,

Today was a sunny day in Canada. I had a surprising email and I was very suspicious. However, I opened it and it was an invitation to my favourite dance class, Abby Lee. I asked my mum if we could go and she said yes. It took ten minutes to get there. I was excited because I have danced all my life. I asked my mum why it took ten minutes but she could not hear me so I left it. Once we got to Abby Lee's dance team she was very mean but I did not care, I danced my heart out about ten times. One time I danced with the team.

Then it was ten o'clock and we went home. I went on my mum's phone and I got an email. I got in. I was very happy but I did not tell my mum until we got home and had a KFC. She was happy.

Chelsey Webster (10)
Coppull Primary School And Children's Centre, Coppull

The Diary Of Amy Houghton

Dear Diary,

Today was so unexpected. I woke up, got ready and called my boyfriend who has brown hair, brown eyes and loves kids. He got to mine and brought me some chocolate and a beautiful bouquet of flowers. We had a cup of coffee and hopped into the car. We got to my sister's house (Sophia) and knocked on the door.

Thirty minutes later I went upstairs to check on my sister and tell her lunch was ready. She came downstairs with me behind until... I missed a step! Luckily, she got to the bottom while I was tumbling down. I couldn't feel my arm and Sophia called my dad. They rushed me to the hospital in ten minutes and showed them my arm. Now I'm stuck in a hospital bed writing my diary.

Amy H.

Sophia Houghton (9)

Coppull Primary School And Children's Centre, Coppull

The Diary Of Arabella

Dear Diary,

Today was full of twists and turns. I was sitting down on my couch while reading a new book from my local library. Everything was going well until my parents and I heard a loud, hard knock on the front door. It was only nine in the morning so I thought it was a bit peculiar. I slowly opened the door to see a tall, royal guard at the door. He then announced that I was the long-lost princess. My heart was racing. I felt shocked, surprised and confused. Was I really a princess? Soon after, my so-called parents said they were the heads of a gang. That was the most surprising day of my life.

Evie Corner (10)
Coppull Primary School And Children's Centre, Coppull

The Diary Of Oliver

Dear Diary,

Today was crazy. I was at school just doing my work in class and the most unexpected thing happened. School finished early so I went down the windy country road. A white van was behind me. It then was in front of me. All of a sudden the people in the white van pulled me in. I was scared, horrified, worried and terrified. I decided to be cheeky and try to cut the ropes. I wasn't able to do it, however, I remember I had a pocketknife. I freed myself, although I pretended I was tied up to the wall. Suddenly, I jumped out of the van and sprinted as quickly as a cheetah back to my house.

Oliver Leather (10)
Coppull Primary School And Children's Centre, Coppull

The Diary Of Grandpa Terry

Dear Diary,

Today was the scariest day of my life. I had woken up and sat on my bed for at least ten minutes. It was 10:30 so I decided to go downstairs to get something to eat. Afterwards, I set off to pick up my granddaughter to go to the shops with her. However, I saw a person in a black van who asked if I would like a ride so I said yes. But I had made a mistake, he was kidnapping me. I was lucky I had my phone on me. I called Hope to help me. She jumped in the window and cut me free. We both ran home safe and sound.

I hope tomorrow will be a better day...

Hope Appleby (10)

Coppull Primary School And Children's Centre, Coppull

The Diary Of Lacey

Dear Diary,

Today was a very bad day and a very angry day. The reason it was a bad day is that I broke my arm and it is very sore. I am pretty sure if I didn't break my arm then it would be a good diary page. I am so annoyed because I didn't get my ice cream like my mum promised. However, when I did get my ice cream after two hours I didn't eat it all so I gave some to my annoying sister. When it was time for bed my mum cut my nightie sleeve and used couch pillows for my arm on my bed. Let's hope tomorrow is better...

Lacey Harrison (10)

Coppull Primary School And Children's Centre, Coppull

The Diary Of A Rugby Player

Dear Diary,

Today I was playing a rugby match against the best team we have ever played against so before the game started I knew it was going to be tough. During the game some of our players were getting injured and our best players, which was really bad for us. We were only just scraping the lead. I knew I was going to be the next person injured so I was getting ready. What do you know? I pulled my hamstring. I was devastated and in pain. I went home and got told I was out for ten weeks til it got better. Now I just sit in bed.

Finley Pearce (9)
Coppull Primary School And Children's Centre, Coppull

The Diary Of Tyler

Dear Diary,

Today is Friday and I am exhausted from the week and can't wait until the weekend comes. I really don't want to go to school so I am skipping it. I started to walk to school and when I got there I started to think about what I should do. I decided to skip it, it was the first time I skipped school. It was scary. I went to a shop and got some food. Then I was on my way to the park when a masked man kidnapped me and took me somewhere but luckily the car broke down. I untied myself, escaped and ran home.

Tyler Wood (9)

Coppull Primary School And Children's Centre, Coppull

The Diary Of A Rich Girl

Dear Diary,
Today I woke up and felt amazing because I had one million pounds so I could finally get the new fabulous trampoline. I told my dad after lunch that I got the largest trampoline and he shouted at me for getting it. My friend came around and we went on the trampoline. She told me to do a backflip because I landed on my right arm and broke it. I was in pain for the rest of the day, although I got a green cast and got a KFC for my first tea with a cast on. Let's hope tomorrow is a better day...

Georgie Stanworth (10)
Coppull Primary School And Children's Centre, Coppull

Lilah And Her Cheeky Sisters

Dear Diary,

Today I woke up and decided to go and play outside since it was a very beautiful and sunny day. However, I tripped over a kerb unexpectedly. Suddenly, I felt I was being lifted up by someone mysterious. I then got chucked into a dark, gloomy and smelly van. Something very strange started to happen. The driver took a very sharp turn at the speed of light back into my street. He told me to get out. I said, "I hope that never happens again."

Lily-Grace Thorley (10)

Coppull Primary School And Children's Centre, Coppull

The Diary Of Missy

Dear Diary,
Today, Missy, my friend was bored and she came to my house but she was kidnapped by a man all in black in a white van. She was taken to a warehouse and me, Oliver, sprinted to the warehouse to get Missy. Missy was freed. When we got home, I gave her food and she went to bed. Me and my owner went upstairs, ate some snacks and played games. We stayed up all night, then went to bed. I wonder what will happen tomorrow. I hope it's fun.

Alfie Wilkinson (9)
Coppull Primary School And Children's Centre, Coppull

The Diary Of Bevan French

Dear Diary,

You will not believe the day I had. I woke up and I made my way over to the DW Stadium. I then went to the changing rooms to get ready. However, I fell into a huge hole. I shouted for help but no one heard. By this time the match had nearly started and someone started looking for me. I shouted for help again. This time they heard me and came over to help. I was pulled out and the match started. I hope tomorrow is better...

Alex Wilson (10)

Coppull Primary School And Children's Centre, Coppull

The Diary Of Bubbles

Dear Diary,

Today my brother (Dunkin) and I were climbing on the tree and the rocks that our owner gave us. I was so happy until the cage started to crack and smash until, *crash!* The cage broke on me and my brother. My brother and I rushed onto the wet, soggy and damp carpet. I hated it so much and I wanted to have my cage back. However, when I looked around I didn't see my brother, he had run off.

Bethany Ashby (10)
Coppull Primary School And Children's Centre, Coppull

The Diary Of Oscar

Dear Diary,

I went outside for a walk around. I was walking like I always do when I saw a newly built road. I went down it and saw a park big enough for my cat body. All of a sudden, I didn't know where I was. I got scared and started walking around. When I saw a road that looked familiar to the one I just walked down I started walking and walking until I knew where I was. I was home.

Lewis Prescott (10)

Coppull Primary School And Children's Centre, Coppull

Daisy The Dancer

Dear Diary,

I woke up this morning and I was excited and ready for the dancing competition at school. I walked through my house door and I was off to my school. I got on the bus and at that moment I reached school and got changed into my outfit. I went onto the stage and did my routine. I even saw my parents in the audience.

Emily Fairhurst (10)

Coppull Primary School And Children's Centre, Coppull

The Diary Of Reuben

Dear Diary,

Today I went to school. At break time Robby walked up to me. I told him I didn't want to be his friend but he chased me around the playground for fifteen whole minutes. At lunchtime, he begged to be my friend again! I said no but eventually, I said yes. Who knows what tomorrow will bring...?

Reuben Nice (9)

Coppull Primary School And Children's Centre, Coppull

Diary Of The Rock

Dear Diary,

Today was a sunny day in LA when I woke up and went to brush my teeth. I got on with my six-hour routine, working on my calf muscles, biceps and stamina. After that, I had a large portion of oats and a beverage of apple juice. I felt exhausted and watched a YouTube video.

Ryan Cooper (10)
Coppull Primary School And Children's Centre, Coppull

Ozzy's Dream

Dear Diary,

Last night I had a dream that my family went on holiday. I was so anxious because my family was going to put me in the kennels. I was worried about going because they were barking at me so aggressively so I thought they were going to hurt me. As I walked through the gates the dogs were in cages and they were still barking at me. When I got put in my cage the owner of the dog kennels opened another dog's cage and the dog ran at me! That was when I woke up from my dream and when I went downstairs I cuddled in with my family. See you soon.

Jessica Campbell (11)
Deaf Hill Primary School, Trimdon Station

The Worst Day Of My Life

Dear Diary,

Today was the worst day ever (well is). I'm stuck in the middle of the forest, and I don't know how to get out. I've probably been here for two hours and something is coming up to me...

Maggie Pearl Duffey (10)

Deaf Hill Primary School, Trimdon Station

Shrek/Alien Takeover

Dear Diary,

Last night something terrifying happened. I peered through my curtains and what I saw flabbergasted me. I saw a lab and in the lab, I saw a horrendous creature and then I saw a big board which said: 'Plan: Take over the world'. After that, I sprinted into my parents' room and shouted, "Argh, there is a monster!"

My parents rushed in and nothing was there so my parents went back in their room. I proceeded to sleep. In the morning I went downstairs and it said: 'Breaking news... There has been a character going around who is named Shrek/Alien. He has a lab and there have been numerous spottings of him'. "We can see him right now, argh!" I said. "Why has the signal gone?" But then I realised he was attacking and now nobody dared to step foot outside. Now important buildings all over the world have been destroyed it was horrendous. I was terrified. I had a look on the Internet and I spotted that he looked lonely so I felt so brave. I went outside and asked him, "Do you want to be my friend?" And after that, all went well.

Finn Devereux (10)
Lugwardine Primary Academy, Bartestree

Hermione And The Troll

Dear Diary,

Today was a bizarre day. It started off with me being early for school at exactly 7am like I usually am. It isn't anything special, it's just me going to the most heavenly place on the school campus... the library. It's so I get my one-hour reading time of my favourite book that I'm so into right now (I was living in paradise). Anyways, that flew by. I started to make my way to my first class of the day which is potions. Although I love learning, potions are not my cup of tea because of our teacher, Professor Snape. And of course, as soon as I set foot in the classroom Snape hit Neville with another long lecture about letting his frog loose for the thousandth time. It wasn't his fault! Anyway, the lesson started off with me searching for the unicorn hair but I was soon interrupted by a deafening sound. *Bang! Roar!* Disaster had struck. A troll had invaded. It was destroying everything. Our whole class rushed to the great hall in a panic but unfortunately, I was in the wrong place at the wrong time and so were my friends. My life was about to go right in front of me until Weasley saved me by shouting, "Petrificus totalus!"

I never thought that would happen, Ron saving me, are you being serious but I may as well take the chance. Yes, that's right. "Avada Kedavra!"
We won fighting a troll. Wow! And after that fight, we went back to our dorms and had a good sleep.

Eva Brown (10)
Lugwardine Primary Academy, Bartestree

The Incredible Diary Of Harry Potter

Dear Diary,

It's me again, Harry. Something terrible has happened. Me and my friends, Hermione, Ron, Luna, Neville and Ginny were eating lunch in the great hall. All of a sudden, the girls needed to go to the loo or as Ron calls it the pee pee poopoo place but it had been a while since they went so Ron and Neville went to look for them. I was feeling really bored but happy because I had some peace and quiet away from Ron, right up until Draco came over and told me I looked like a troll and that trolls can't play quidditch. I just turned him into a ferret.

After a while, I started to get a bit worried so I went to look for them in the girls' bathroom. Something terrible happened. Bellatrix and Greyback had all my friends tied up and were flying away with them but suddenly Luna dropped her shoe. It had a note in it. It said: 'Harry, go to Dumbledore and say 'blueberry', he will know what to do'.

I felt so eager to go and talk to Dumbledore but I knew we had to go to our dorms. In the middle of the night, I woke up sweating. I had been sweating all night because of this dream I had about Voldemort torturing my friends at the ministry. I will write again soon when this is all over.

Molly Lewis (10)
Lugwardine Primary Academy, Bartestree

The Incredible Diary Of Slimer Gamer

Dear Diary,

The BFF heart got taken in by the evil versions of us. I felt worried. The evil versions of myself and Stripes stole the heart in a town called BFF Topia in a galaxy far away from Earth. If you don't know, I'm Slimer Gamer and my best friend is Stripes who is the last tiger in the universe. I'm half slime, half man and I am two feet tall. On the 2nd of July, the BFF heart was stolen. Stripes and I spent about a week looking for the ship of evil versions of ourselves. We followed the ship across galaxies. We managed to infiltrate the ship through a window as we were so small. I slipped through a vent, made some noise to distract the guards and then walked down the corridor. The heart was in storage in the core of the ship and was easy to get. But as soon as we touched it an alarm went off. I put a fake heart in its place and ran. I felt scared in case we didn't make it in time. We pressed the self-destruct button in the steering area and found a hatch at the bottom of the ship.

The ship went boom! but we escaped. What a relief. We came back home and Stripes and I had a party.

Bram Brand (9)

Lugwardine Primary Academy, Bartestree

Mega Morales

Dear Diary,

Today was a great day. I was just sitting on my sofa at home waiting for Santa but then my Spidy senses went off so I suited up to go save the day. But then I saw Tom Holland. "Tom, go away!" I shouted.

"No! I want to save the day!" he said.

But I wouldn't accept that so I started to swing as fast as possible. But when we got there, Venom and Carnage had already saved the day. With this being so we all went home and relaxed on my sofa and watched TV. While eating snacks until I went to bed. In the morning, I ate my favourite thing, Spideyos, for breakfast. Next, I went to school where it was infested by ants. For more info read Lexi's diary!

Anyway, back to my story, at school we have air-ups, that's an investigation Lexi's on by the way. The air-ups went missing so I have to use a school cup instead. They are icky because other people use them for themselves, so selfish! But after school, this guy walked up to me and said all the air-ups were hidden in the headmaster's office so I went to get them and when got them I was done.

James Green (10)

Lugwardine Primary Academy, Bartestree

My Secret Of Titanic

Dear Diary,

My trip on Titanic was amazing. The first step that I took on it, it was like the shiny bar had never been used. The floors had never been touched and the walls smelt of fresh daisies and I felt at home but the day that me and my family all had breakfast but something didn't feel right even though I felt at home. All they talked about was money so I needed to get away. I ran to the edge of the boat and held my breath in the fresh air thinking to myself, *it's going to get better.* But then, *crash, bang!* An iceberg straight ahead scraped the boat and the people below deck ran to escape the flooding down there but then the water rose into half of the boat and then, *snap!* The boat broke in half and then, *snap!* The boat broke in half and sank. Luckily the lifeboats saved quite a few lives but only the rich not the poor. Then both of the boats went down to the bottom of the sea and all we could see were cold faces burning in frost and I was the only human still standing but then the boats found me and I survived.

Flo Scott (10)
Lugwardine Primary Academy, Bartestree

SpongeBob Discovers A New Jellyfish

Dear Diary,

Today was amazing... Actually, wait, let's start from the beginning. This morning, I woke up and was super excited because I ordered a new jelly fishing net and on the website, it said: 'Best jelly fishing net ever'. It was super good at catching jellyfish, but it didn't come. After waiting for 20 minutes I remembered that I ordered it to be delivered to my work. So I went to work and after serving 221 crabs, fish and every other crustation and sea creature (and waiting 15 minutes) I heard a knock on the back door. "Hello, a delivery for... SpongeBob SquarePants," said a delivery fish. "Yep, that's me, thank you very much," I said so I went to the jelly fishing field. After 10 minutes I caught 2 blue, 10 purple, 1 yellow, 6 pink and 2 orange jellyfish but then I saw a jellyfish that was blue, purple and pink! So I tried to catch it, but I missed. But because I am always positive I tried again and caught it! I have never seen it in my jellyfishing book before, so I've discovered a new jellyfish!

Monty Cutter (10)

Lugwardine Primary Academy, Bartestree

32

School Life

Dear Diary,
Yesterday was crazy, so I was getting ready to go to my new school. I ate my breakfast, did my hair, brushed my teeth then got in the car. When I arrived I saw like over 1,000 cars in the car park! I said bye to my mum and then entered the building... When I walked in the whole corridor went quiet. When I opened the door, I went to my class (silence). Someone lifted the table (they weren't touching it!). A boy named Mark said to me, "I will show you your power tomorrow!"
I was shocked! The next day I woke up extra early and went to school. I saw Mark and I ran over to him. He whispered, "Oh hi again. Are you ready to find out what your power is?"
"Yes!" I screamed.
He slowly said, "Just say 'igoola boogala hip dop hop' then just say where you want to go. If you wanna go back then just repeat."
Surprisingly I teleported! And that was my crazy school day.

Milla Pajak (10)
Lugwardine Primary Academy, Bartestree

The Incredible Diary Of Phillip Richardson

Dear Diary,
Life is rubbish, I'm currently in prison writing with a toothpick on a wall. It's an old used one as well. The year is currently 2113 and when I was a kid I was a huge show-off. My parents would buy me fake branded shoes and clothes and I would show off about it. Then, when I turned 18 I started my business called Clothes 'N' Stuff and I earned millions. I was so rich and wealthy but the crazy thing was... I still wore fake brands still! Called Mike, Oddidas and Luma! I was also still a show-off and then suddenly I heard a buzz. It was my phone. My friend was calling me. I answered and he said, "Look at the news!" I turned it on and... *Boom!* I was on the news! Let's just say it wasn't a good thing. They found out that I wear fake brands. I was horrified, terrified, petrified. They even found out I went robbing a fake clothes shop. That's how I ended up in jail.

Huxley Corbett (10)
Lugwardine Primary Academy, Bartestree

The Incredible Diary Of Ava

Dear Diary,

Today has been the weirdest/coolest day ever. Let me tell you all about it. So I woke up this morning and I totally forgot about my competition until my mum said, "Remember you have a trampolining comp today."

So I got in the car and we went to the comp. Mum said, "We need to stop off to get your new trampolining shoes."

I said, "Okay."

It must have been 20 minutes before we got there. "Can you get out of the car and go into the shop?" Mum said.

So I began to walk into the shop. Suddenly, it was a whole new world. The shop now looked all colourful and magical. I asked the man if they had any trampolining shoes. He said, "Yes, I think this pair will be good."

I said, "Thank you," and went out of the shop and turned back to normal.

I went to my comp and came first. From now on I will always wear these shoes.

Belle Ryder (10)

Lugwardine Primary Academy, Bartestree

The Incredible Diary Of Spider-Man

Dear Diary,

Today was weird but okay. I was enjoying my day and it was going very well until a portal came. It was right in front of me. So like any other person, I went in. It was okay but when I saw Spider-Man it made my day better. He gave me a black and red Spider-Man suit that definitely made my day. The portal finished and it took us to Jurassic World. So we started swinging but we saw Venom and Carnage. "Why are you here?" said Spidy.

"To get the gem," Venom said.

"Why?"

We said, "It controls the world."

"We can't let them get it," Spidy said.

So we ran through the jungle and we got there. But they were there first so we ran after them but there was a T-rex so we webbed it up. We caught up. We got the gem and then webbed them up. We didn't know what to do so we smashed it. We went home and celebrated.

Ollie Bryan (10)
Lugwardine Primary Academy, Bartestree

The Incredible Diary Of Steve

Dear Diary,
This morning the strangest thing happened. I woke up, opened my wardrobe and suddenly I got teleported to a jungle! I was so confused about how I got there, but that didn't bother me. I just wanted to explore. I started to walk through the jungle. Suddenly I saw something, it was a monkey. It started swinging, I waved goodbye as it swung away. I then continued my journey. As I went on I saw a snake, it was hissing quite loudly. As I was continuing my journey I saw loads and loads of little insects so I got out my magnifying glass to take a closer look. They looked so interesting. When I looked up I saw loads of beautiful birds, they were all tweeting and it sounded so relaxing. As I was enjoying it I got teleported back home. I wonder what will happen tomorrow?

Sam Dutton (10)
Lugwardine Primary Academy, Bartestree

The Incredible Diary Of Simon

The day has come. I'm making history. 1972. I am going to be eating the world. That's right, I'm eating the world. I'm starting at... Hmmm, aha! France. Well, this is going to take a long time. Oh well, I'm going to start eating now.
One year later, I'm travelling to England. This is going to take a long time to get there on a ferry. I just remembered I'm seasick so in my opinion, I should be on a plane. Finally, I'm here.
Seven months later, the next country. Only two more countries to go. Canada. I'm so tired. It's 8pm already. Oh my goodness, maple syrup. Yes. One year later, final one. Austria. Yes. Time ticks. Cake. They even have so much pastry. Done.
Oh, I need to get to a rock to survive. Nooo! I have no friends.

Rowan Price Gough (10)
Lugwardine Primary Academy, Bartestree

The Diary Of The World

50 years ago there was a mad scientist called Igor. His whole name is Igor Enidrawgul and he discovered a remarkable thing but the scientist that discovered it was evil... Now! Hey guys sorry about that it was like a normal day... We went to school. The Avenger saved the day, there were lots of earthquakes wait, what... oh... okay... well I think we know who's making the earthquakes. Well, it was that big fella and that old guy Igor created him. His name is Demoned, and Igor created lots of zombies too. Oh no! Guess what happened... Demoned just broke out and all the zombies too. The Avengers will save us, oh wait, the guy is huge so you know what they did. They called all The Avengers and they dominated him and all the zombies too and we never got bothered by him again.

Jacob Jones (10)
Lugwardine Primary Academy, Bartestree

The Incredible Diary Of... Jacob Wheadon

Dear Diary,

I have officially done it, I am victorious in the cup. I will tell you about it... So first it was the warm-up. We did a marking game where you have to stay close to your partner. But they run away from you in a crowded rectangle area. Then we also had a team talk and I found out I was on the bench. Also, the game kicked off and five minutes later we scored a free kick. 1-0. We played well and then I came on and got a free kick. I hit it and it skimmed the crossbar. Also, I have to say nothing happened until after halftime and we got an opportunity. 2-0. And then a tap in. 3-0. Then our player was through on goal and then the goalkeeper took him out. Penalty! 4-0. Full-time and we did it. We did it! It went insane.

Jacob Wheadon (10)
Lugwardine Primary Academy, Bartestree

The Incredible Diary Of...

Dear Diary,

75 years ago, in Victorian times, a girl, Lacey, aka me, got into the palace. I was very shy and I was a daughter of a guard for Queen Victoria. One rainy day my dad, Darren, took me to the palace. I was petrified! It was so big and fancy and tidy, my room could never be this tidy. Then Victoria spoke. "Guards, there is an invader, get them!"

My dad and all the other guards ran off leaving me with the Queen. "Hello your royal highness," I whispered as I bowed.

She looked and asked me who I was. I told her my name and my backstory. She got my dad and told him to send me home at once. When I got home I thought about my adventure. No one will believe me. That's all for now. Bye!

Milly Jones (10)

Lugwardine Primary Academy, Bartestree

The Diary Of A Cursed Wizard

Dear Diary,
Today was another day in prison. Wait, did I say prison? I meant school! Anyway as usual I was late and of course, as soon as I set foot in my first class Professor Snape hit me with the defining sound of a good telling-off. Finally, after a while, I was walking full of pride to my last class before lunch. But not for long, of course, my eyes had to meet Crabbe and Goyle, the school bullies. They must have been in a good mood because this time they gave me an option. After class, Professor McGonagall gave me my test complete with grade, obviously, it was an F. And no surprise as soon as I put my battered shoe inside the lunch hall a blob of mashed potato hit my face. Well, wish me good luck for tomorrow.

Lois Griffiths (10)
Lugwardine Primary Academy, Bartestree

My Mum's Birthday

Dear Diary,

I have just got back from the Cock of Tupsley pub and I am going to write all about it. I will tell you all the names by the way. My mum's sisters are called Helen and Sarah and of course myself. My family's names are Jean and Jeff, they are my nan and grandad. My mum's mum and my Auntie Sara, Lowie and Chloe, Helen and Huw, Molly, Isla, my sister, Rosie and me. The kids played and the grown-ups shouted and drank beer and talked whilst opening presents. We ate food and had lots of fun. Then we went down the pole, it was so fun. We went upside down in a handstand. My mum, who was having the best time ever, absolutely loved it. She said to me when we got home that she loved her birthday.

Evie Blackwell (9)
Lugwardine Primary Academy, Bartestree

The Incredible Diary Of A Magical Dream

Dear Diary,

Last night I had a magical dream. As soon as I drifted off to sleep my magic dream began. I had a vision I was in a world of sweets, it was the best! The trees were candyfloss and there were chocolate rivers and lollipop flowers. I was in heaven! Suddenly, I turned around and I saw the most beautiful horse ever. I was amazed. Then I heard a voice that made me jump. It was the horse asking if I would like a ride. Of course, I said yes! I hopped on the horse's back and off we went. We galloped across fields of sweets. Annoyingly my mum woke me up because I had to go to school and we were running late. I blame Mum really. Thanks for listening. I will write tomorrow.

Amber Hewlett (10)

Lugwardine Primary Academy, Bartestree

The Incredible Diary Of Andrew

Dear Diary,

I found a pen on the floor. I thought it was a normal pen but it was a secret spy pen in London. Really it was a spy pen with a spy camera on it. I looked at it and saw a camera I looked it up on the Internet and found out it was a spy pen. The spy, Agent 365, found me and told me about an evil villain trying to take over Planet Earth. Agent 365 knew where Zorbavor was and told me where Zorbavor lived - a normal flat in London. I found his flat, I planted the pen on his desk so it showed everything in the room. Zorbavor said, "I'm going to Big Ben."

Agent 365 and I were one step ahead and we caught Zorbavor at Big Ben and saved Planet Earth.

Billy Edwards (9)
Lugwardine Primary Academy, Bartestree

The Sprout That Went Missing

Dear Diary,

Today a sprout of mine went missing. You're probably thinking, like a sprout, that's not important. But it really is, it gives me superpowers. I saw it go into the river and the river is massive! So I jumped in to find it. I saw a giant shark that had it in its mouth. I was so upset but a mermaid came from behind! I didn't know mermaids were real! The mermaid grabbed my superhero sprout out of the shark's mouth. The mermaid made it back to her cave and I ran home with happiness and I made it home just in time for dinner. I am so happy because of that mermaid and she risked her life just to get my sprout. I hope I see her again.

Maisie Pockett (10)

Lugwardine Primary Academy, Bartestree

The Incredible Diary Of Stripes

Dear Diary,

Today was different! I woke up on a sandy bed as a girl and a boy stood above me. They told me that me and my friends got attacked and I was the only survivor.

We all got on a boat and went to see Scaredy Cat and Cursed Slimergamer. We went to get the BFF's heart! We had tried to get it before but this time we got the heart no problem... until the cursed Slimergamer found us!

We escaped. We got to safety and arrived at my house. It had been turned into a giant statue of me! I'm also now in the BFF gang. I now also have the power of speed! And there's more... but that's for another day.

From Stripes.

Josh Stollery (10)
Lugwardine Primary Academy, Bartestree

Garry Finds Freedom

Dear Diary,

I'm a fish called Garry and I was so bored of being just a random fish in a teeny tiny tank. I wanted freedom, I really did. I didn't have any friends either. I mean what was I supposed to do when I was just stuck in a lonely tank? "Oh I have an idea," I said aloud. "I'm going to escape this old town." So I flopped out of my tank and tried and tried until I got to the sea.

Finally, I found the sea, it was amazing. I could just swim and swim. After I swam for a bit I found a fish called Larry. He and I got along so well, so we became really good friends.

Henry Grimshaw (9)

Lugwardine Primary Academy, Bartestree

The Ants

Dear Diary,

Hi, I'm Lexi, today has been crazy. There were naughty ants in our school and they went into everyone's bags but nobody knew until we all went to our bags. There were ants everywhere. There were some on the pegs, on bags, even on our air-ups and then... We saw the queen ant! She was massive and all of the other ants were getting food for the queen. The worst thing happened. The ants started to come into our classroom. Everyone was screaming but something happened. The ants went so everyone went to go and find them but really I know they are going to be back for revenge.

Rosie Anderson (10)

Lugwardine Primary Academy, Bartestree

A Day In My Life

Dear Diary,

I went to my friend's house then we went to McDonald's and we had food. After that, we went to the cinema and we took pictures of someone's balloons. Next, me and my friend ran to screen 2, chose our seats and started chatting and spilling gossip. So then we were watching the new Matilda movie. Suddenly we needed the toilet. We had been in there for ten minutes and chatting together. Then we went out to watch the movie. We knew what happened in the movie and so we continued to watch all of it.

Nicole Solska (10)

Lugwardine Primary Academy, Bartestree

Dalia's Sassy Dance Concert

Dear Diary,

I was so excited because I had a dance concert. I was nervous/excited. I was going to perform in front of 700 or so people. I was so scared. After I got changed I got in my friend's car and we went to the place. It was massive! Some girls were getting their hair done. My friend said, "I want to get my hair done," but sadly we couldn't. Then someone said to line up and we all ran to go line up. They told us all the people would watch us dance. Then they started to call up classes to practice on the stage. Then it was our turn so we went and danced on the stage. We got all warmed up. Then some ladies did our hair. It looked stunning, it was a plated ponytail. Then they put on red lipstick, but we had to wait 20 minutes before we performed. We had two dances. We did them one by one. Once we finished we had to wait another 20 minutes to do our next dance. When I went home my parents said they were so proud of me. And that is the story of my sassy dance concert!

Dalia Belilo (8)
Nancy Reuben Primary School, London

Who Found The Magic Key?

Dear Diary,

I was playing with my rabbit, Lili. I had lots of fun. Then suddenly I saw a magic door. I went in with Lily and, *bang!* We were in a rainforest. It was so pretty with lots of flowers. Well, I had nothing to do there so I just walked and walked and then I saw talking animals. I screamed so loud like a bee had stung me. But my rabbit could also speak but I never knew that my rabbit could speak. So I found out that my rabbit could speak. I tried to talk to the animals but they were too shy.

Me and Lily found a mystery map and it said: 'Find the key so then you can go back to your city'. I got so excited to go back to the city. So I tried to find the key but I couldn't find it. I was screaming all day but then the animals told me that they were going to find it with me. I was so happy. We kept on looking for the key. Then suddenly I found another map. It said: 'If you don't beat the time you will stay in the rainforest forever'. I got so scared, there were only five minutes left. "Oh no, what are we supposed to do?"

The animals told me, "We have to find it, now!"

Me and the animals were looking so hard but then guess what, Lili found the key! I was so proud. We opened the door and we were back to our city and that was the end of my day.

Tehila Babaev (8)
Nancy Reuben Primary School, London

The Biggest Splash

Dear Diary,

I was on the top and... Let's start from the beginning. Hi, my name is Nova. I'm 23 years old and I am an Olympic diver. I compete for England. Recently, I was in a competition in Sydney, Australia. I got into the finals! I carefully climbed up the steep ladder, got up at the top and stood up straight. I got ready to jump and smashed my leg on the diving board! The paramedics came straight away. I was rushed to the hospital immediately. The doctors gave me an X-ray and found out I had paralysed my leg. Although I was going to miss diving, I was way too scared to dive again. When the doctors gave me permission, I climbed into the deep, blue water to swim. I was really good at swimming. I signed up for some competitions and won! I became a Paralympic swimmer and became famous. And that's my story for you.

Nava Brownstein (8)

Nancy Reuben Primary School, London

The Nightmare

Dear Diary,

Yesterday I had an awful nightmare. It all began when I went to the circus. I went there to cheer Mr Eli on. "The first act of the night is Mr Eli."
"Whoo! Go Mr Eli!"
He came onto the stage on a huge beach ball. He had tennis balls and started to juggle. He started to do tricks and after the first trick, his tennis balls fell onto the floor. He fell off the beach ball. He was crying and when he was walking off stage he tripped over the tennis balls and landed in a tunnel. He jumped out of the tunnel and landed on a football pitch. I must have gone in the tunnel too because I was on the football pitch. Everyone was staring at us. We ducked and went into another tunnel. All of the ends closed and we were stuck in the tunnel, just me and Mr Eli...

Sofia Carr (8)
Nancy Reuben Primary School, London

First Spaceship Ever

Dear Diary,
I have a lot of homework to do but I've already done one page. I'm really looking forward to my birthday because my mum's getting me a telescope. It's almost 5pm and I just finished dinner. It was a chicken burger with cucumber. On my birthday I got my telescope. One night I was doing my homework when I heard something rattling in the sky. I opened my window, looked through my telescope and there was a lot of metal flying towards me! I shoved my telescope onto my bed. I ducked near my cupboard. It landed with a big crash. I heard my mum coming to my room. I shoved the metal under my bed, shut my window and pretended to sleep. Every morning I built a spaceship step by step, with the metal. One morning I finally finished it. I told the news and I became famous.

Sam Rosten (8)
Nancy Reuben Primary School, London

Football Mad

Dear Diary,

I was playing in football training when, on purpose, someone kicked my ankle and it really hurt. I was really sad because the finals were the next day and I had hurt my ankle. I couldn't play in the finals. Also, when I was playing at Anfield training ground, I saw that the person who kicked my ankle was on my team and I knew why he did it. It was because I was about to score a goal and he kicked my ankle so he could score the goal... and that's how I hurt my ankle.

Joshy Black (8)
Nancy Reuben Primary School, London

The Unplanned Football Game

Dear Diary,

It was the middle of a football game but we heard thunder and lightning so the game ended. Since it was France, Mbappé was still training and the coach called him in. The players were angry. One hour later the stadium was flooded as well as the changing rooms. Everyone was terrified. What will happen next... Will the game carry on in another stadium? Maybe. Maybe not. I'll tell you next time.

Adam Abramowitz (8)

Nancy Reuben Primary School, London

My World Cup Diary

Dear Diary,

I am Roge Milla, part of the Cameroon 1990 squad. Would you like me to tell you my story? Okay, so it all started in Milan against Argentina. They had amazing players like Maradona. When the match started the Argentina fans were calling us names so that's when we got furious. In the space of 20 minutes, three players were booked. At half-time, it was 0-0.

After 49 minutes Biyik got a red card and then another player but then Mfede crossed to Biyik who scored. 1-0 Cameroon. After that, the whistle blew. We went wild. Next up was the Soviet Union. We were weaker than them and Bell, Mfede, Biyik and I weren't playing so it went 1-0, 2-0, 3-0... 4-0. Next Columbia, we were against Higuita. After 27 minutes he was tackled by Mfede who scored. 1-0 Cameroon. Then I scored and they blew the whistle. 2-0. Next, I scored against Romania. 1-0 whistle!

Then England. Unfortunately, we lost.

Diego Catavello Ron (8)
Redfield Educate Together Primary Academy, Redfield

The Floating School

Dear Diary,

I was having a normal day then I went to class. During class, we had to line up for a lecture. In the middle of Professor Kean's announcements, the school started floating up, up, up! Everyone was floating in the air. Suddenly I felt a tickle on my back. Just at that moment, wings burst out and my uniform turned into an angel's dress then my hair turned into platinum blonde angelic curls (this is where my adventure starts).

I started seeing gates for Heaven and I flew out. Everybody was bowing down to me and my adventure started here. In the blink of an eye, I went to the outside world. Above the clouds I flew, spreading kindness to communities, city by city. The government heard about this and was mesmerised and made an announcement that said, "If you are kind and helpful you will pay less tax." When I heard this I was on cloud 9, it was the best thing in my life. Obviously, the kindness and empathy paid off. During my celestial travels, I encountered breathtaking unknown species. From vibrant, jaw-dropping plants to ethereal creatures with delicate wings and feathers as bright as vibrant colours. Each encounter brought a sense of awe and joy. This was the best thing in my life.

There were also lush forests and crystal clear waters. I made the creatures feel welcome on Earth and grew a bond with each and every creature.

Sanaa Mohamed (8)
Redfield Educate Together Primary Academy, Redfield

The Hole Of Doom

An extract

Dear Diary,
Today I had a stressful time. It started off as a nice simple jump over a hole. I say 'hole' but it was the hole of doom! No cat had ever gone in and come out again. The entrance wasn't big, it was the size of a manhole cover. I did it for my friends, Twinkle and Carmel. They get so excited about a tiny jump. If I haven't told you who I am, I'm Kenya and I'm four years old. They say I'm a kitten but I'm actually an adult. I am a black and white cat, and my owner loves me. My nickname is Kenya the Cool if you're wondering. Anyway, I paced myself and well, I said this... Meow (not in celebration!). I was falling. I mean, what would you say if you were a cat who'd fallen in a thousand-foot ditch (actually, by my skills in mathematics it was twenty-four purrometres).
Then I hit the ground. I felt like I'd fainted for a while, then suddenly I woke up. And staring at me right in the eyes, were 30 other cats. Suddenly one chirped, "I'm Thistle, hi."
Another said, "I'm Alice."

Another... "I'm Todd."

Finally, the last one bellowed, "I'm Sunshine. What brings you to the hole of Actunsac?"...

Eve Bridgewater (7)

Redfield Educate Together Primary Academy, Redfield

My Mad Day

Dear Diary,

Yesterday, I had a crazy day. It was so chaotic and unpredictable. What was that? Do you want me to tell you about it? Fine. So first, I was getting ready for school and my dad charged in and said, "What are you doing?"

"I am getting dressed, Daddy," I said.

"Getting dressed, getting dressed, what is wrong you, girl!"

So I charged out of the room and went to school on my own. When I got to school my teacher, Mrs Merfey said, "Why are you late, girl?" when I was actually five minutes early, crazy, right?

Finally, my friend, Skyler, came up to me and I thought, *what now?* But actually he said, "What is wrong?"

"Oh..." I said.

"I am talking to you."

"Oh umm... well everything is all a bit wrong today." Then we chatted for hours.

Elliot Colebrook (8)

Redfield Educate Together Primary Academy, Redfield

My Day In Wales

Dear Diary,

On Saturday 10th June 2023 we drove along the motorway for one hour. We went to Aberdare in Wales. We were going to a splash park. There was a lake with pedaloes that looked like swans and dragons. Ducks, swans and geese were in the water and walking around on the path. Me and Meadow dressed up like Moana. We ate party food and sang Happy Birthday with a cake for Meadow. It was really hot. Suddenly it started to rain. I was brave and stayed out in the rain but wore a poncho to keep me dry. We played in the park in the rain.

Elise Reeves (8)
Redfield Educate Together Primary Academy, Redfield

The One Kittypet And Other Stray Cat

Dear Diary,

I was sitting in the forest and heard a noise. It was coming from a tree so I walked a bit closer. Then I looked up and saw another cat. I asked her what her name was and she said, "Katlen!" I asked if she wanted to be friends and she said yes. I told her to come to my house and she looked surprised. I noticed she had no collar on and realised she was a stray. While we were walking to my house, she kept asking me questions. We got to my house and I let her sleep in my bed.

A few days later it was Valentine's Day and I wanted to make something special for someone special. So I got her some flowers and told her I liked her. She said she liked me too and now we're together.

Bailey.

Linda Platore (9)
Ruskin Academy, Wellingborough

Teacher Troubles

Dear Diary,

Yesterday at school was a bad day because no children would listen to me and I forgot my lunch. So I went home and guess what, I forgot my keys so I had to walk. Finally, I was home. I went to bed because I was tired.

Today I walked to school but was not happy about it. I forgot to pack my lunch again. The school was shut. Yay! I headed home as happy as ever. I couldn't believe it.

Bye for now,

Mrs Bailey.

Michaela Ward (9)

Ruskin Academy, Wellingborough

My Amazing Day

Dear Diary,

Today my students were amazing. They treated me like I was their parent. After the holidays they have been perfect little children with big hearts. One even yelled, "I don't want to leave Year 3."
I'm so happy that they're with me, I thought.
Bye for now.
Mr Morris.

Theo White (8)

Ruskin Academy, Wellingborough

My Day

Dear Diary,

Today I was so clumsy that I tripped and all of my food went flying into the air and then landed in my hair. Then I was playing with the skipping rope and after a few seconds, I tangled myself into the skipping rope. I always have bad luck!

Cleopatra Leon (9)

Ruskin Academy, Wellingborough

Eye Wonder?

Dear Diary,

Today was weird at school. We were opening a time capsule buried fifty years ago. My teacher started digging where it was according to the map but it wasn't there. Everyone was disappointed that it couldn't be found. I was surprised that nobody could see it even though it was just a few steps to the left. I told the teacher where it was and everyone wondered how I knew. I said, "I can just see it." Some laughed and some didn't believe me but my teacher dug a hole where I pointed and found the capsule! People stopped laughing and my teacher stared at me in utter shock. They all wanted to know how I knew it would be there. I couldn't explain other than, "I knew it was just there."

My teacher exclaimed, "That's impossible, it's buried nearly four feet deep!"

I thought everyone could see what I saw but obviously not. Some people were staring at me and I could hear some girls muttering the word 'freak' under their breath. I felt embarrassed and different but also powerful! What do I do with this power? Where did it come from? Does anyone else have powers or is it just me? What do I do with this?

Do I use this to help others or for my own good? I really do have some tough decisions to make... don't I...?

Neve Burton (10)

St Ives Junior School, St Ives

Lilly's Lost Pony

Dear Diary,

Today I was walking my dog Lexi down to the yard so I could train for a show on my horse, Lola. But when I got there Lola was gone!

My friend Leah was on a walk in the woods and gave me a phone call saying, "I just found Lola in the woods! Is everything okay?"

I replied, "Yes, I just got to the barn and she was gone!"

Leah walked her back to the barn and I got on and started training.

After three hours of training, I put her to bed and me and Lexi walked back home.

The next day I would have to get up super early so I went straight to bed after getting everything packed. I got everything ready and got into my PJs. When I went to bed Lexi curled up on my chest. My mom came in and said, "Leah is sleeping over because her mom is really busy at work."

So we got her bed set up. When she was in bed we put on a movie. I asked her, "What movie would you like to watch?"

"Please could we watch the Addams Family?"

It was just a few days till Halloween so of course I said yes.
Whilst we were watching the movies I wrote this.
I'll write to you again tomorrow. Now bye!

Lacey Bolton (10)

St Ives Junior School, St Ives

My Adventure To The Magical Land Of Candy!

Dear Diary,

I won! I won! I won the drawing competition and the prize was a night's stay at a magical candy land! I got picked up from my house in a colourful hot air balloon made of ice cream, it had chocolate sauce and sprinkles on it! When I landed there, I saw loads of people getting transported around to their rooms in little taxis with wheels made of doughnuts. This was the most exciting place I have ever seen! It got even better as I got closer to the hotel which looked like a castle made of KitKats, strolling up the rocky road pathways, through the lollipop trees and looking up at the candyfloss clouds, I felt a sensation of butterflies in my tummy! Walking over the chocolate bridges to get across the velvety cocoa rivers, I finally got to my room. My eyes lit up when I saw my bed, fluffy like marshmallows.

That night I soaked in the indulgent white chocolate bath, sipping on a rainbow slushie! I felt overjoyed, delighted and thrilled. I took a big jump into my cosy bed and fell into a deep sleep...

Suddenly, I heard a big bang!
I woke up and I was back in my small town of St Ives in Cornwall! Oh no, this was all a dream!

Staci Vine (10)
St Ives Junior School, St Ives

The Day I Went To Space

Dear Diary,

Today I went to space. Let me tell you! So I was just playing in my back garden when all of a sudden the tree had a hole in it and it looked like space in that hole. I was flabbergasted.

I went up to the hole and stuck my finger through. It disappeared! I pulled my finger back out. I was okay! I thought to myself, *where did my finger go and why did it feel cold when I stuck my finger through?* So I stuck my head through and I could still breathe and talk but was I in space? How could I breathe? I had so many questions but I saw a little boy tied to a large rock and I thought *has he been abducted by aliens?*

So I stepped through completely. The boy had just noticed me so I snuck past the aliens and untied the boy.

"Thank you!" the boy exclaimed. "How could I ever repay you?"

I shushed him. "Come on, the aliens are right there!"

We snuck past and got to the portal. Once we got home he thanked me and was on his way.
Oh, time for tea. Bye!

Pheobe Trevorrow (10)

St Ives Junior School, St Ives

Power Up

Dear Diary,

I'm Milo and I'm the god of... absolutely... nothing! So now you're probably wondering, if I don't have powers how am I a god? Well, let me explain. I'm living in the totally real mythology land of The-Harriet-Definitely-Didn't-Make-This-Up Realm, and my mum and dad are really powerful gods. I don't know why but they have really lame powers, but I can't say anything as I don't have any powers. They have the powers of lips and the power of eyebrows! (I told you it was pretty lame!)

But away from that, my story is about how I got sent from 1520 BC to modern-day New York! Well, it all started when I kind of... cut off the goddess' hair. Hair! So I got punished, blah, blah, blah, got sent to Earth, blah, blah, blah, but it was only once I got to Earth I discovered my power through my love of crisps! I learnt that my power was to make crisps appear! Crazy, right? Because crisps were created after me. I was clearly born in the wrong time period!

Harriet Hooper (10)
St Ives Junior School, St Ives

Fast Craft Zoe

Dear Diary,

Today was very eventful, so let's get started...

8:20am, I was walking to school when I heard a cat meowing. Looking all around, I spotted a smoky, black, scruffy cat that was about to jump from a high branch. As quick as a flash, I weaved a trampoline to catch the frightened cat.

While this was happening a crowd was gathering. Next, I had to spray them with a memory eraser as I had forgotten to put on my mask. Then I found myself running as I was twenty minutes late for school. (How would I explain that to my teacher?!) After making up a lame excuse and just about getting away with it, I sat down ready for maths.

Suddenly the ground quivered. I looked over to my right and saw that Beth was moving away from me with half my class! The school was splitting!

We were sent home immediately which is where I am now writing this. All afternoon the news was covering stories all over the world about similar events.

How am I going to stop this?!

Keavy Devenny (10)
St Ives Junior School, St Ives

Diary Log Day: 3128

Dear Diary,

If you come into the restaurant I work in (as a mere dish-collecting robot) you would think I didn't have much potential. Well... I don't blame you. Every day I pester Sir to let me work in the kitchen but he says that I just need to get on with my job and I am lucky enough as it is. Just last week I asked him if I could spend just one day training with sushi master Hiro Nakamoto in the sushi bar. I (as usual) got a straight no.

You know I've saved over 100 recipes to my memory log alongside all my diary entries? My metal limbs are rusting after pacing all the aisles, collecting everyone's dirty dishes. Really, humans can be so lazy.

Today Sir told me that robots don't cook, they clean. My feelings chip got muddled at this. But anyway, people will be people as our kind has learned. I am going to save you to my memory log now.

Robo.

Kit McAvay (10)

St Ives Junior School, St Ives

My Dad In Hospital

Dear Diary,

I was surfing with my friends, training for a big comp! I could win £10,000!

But when I got back to the beach I had a phone call! My dad was in a car crash! He survived but he needed surgery. It was £5,000 and I knew I had to win.

It was the big day! I surfed my heart out and made it to the finals! The only thing I was thinking about was my dad...

The winners came out from the speaker. I won it! I went straight to the hospital. It went up to £5,500 but I did it!

He is healthy now and will be cheering future comps!

Millie Murt (10)

St Ives Junior School, St Ives

The Missing Pen

Dear Diary,

Today was frightful. If you want to understand the story then I have one thing I need to tell you. I have a magic yellow pen which I carry absolutely everywhere. It creates whatever I write/draw. But today something happened. Listen up...

The morning was fairly normal apart from the fact that I had to draw about five whole bags of dog food for my dog, Daisy. For breakfast, I had scrambled eggs, yoghurt and strawberries. Yum!

It was when I was taking a walk on the beach when it went wrong. I was drawing a triple choc ice cream on my favourite sketchpad. Then suddenly *whoosh!* My pen flew out of my hand, caught by the wind and dropped into the sand. I couldn't find it.

By now, I was as anxious as a guinea pig. What if they used it for evil? I needed to calm down. I licked my Mr Whippy, racking my brain.

Ow! I felt something. I looked down and saw... my pen! I was so happy!

Hope to see you soon,

Bye!

Abigail Macpherson (9)
St Mary Queen Of Martyrs RC Primary School, Hull

Embarrassing Diary

Dear Diary,

I lost my other diary in a pond yesterday, so now I am writing in my new one. Ever since I lost my old one, I have been feeling embarrassed because I put a load of embarrassing things in there, but don't blame me! I hoped no one would find it!

I went to London on Thursday. Me and my mum went to a pond but out of nowhere, my diary slipped out of my bag. I didn't realise that the bag's zipper was open, that's how I lost my old diary.

We went back to the hotel and I noticed a boy swimming and he found my soggy diary. I hid under the hotel bed in embarrassment. The boy was looking in my diary and was laughing like crazy, even though I was lying down in tears...

Next, a group of boys came up to him, took the diary and looked in it. I was terrified.

Me and my mum are home now. I hope they didn't look at page 84, the most embarrassing page ever...

See you soon.

Lilly Kate Harrison (9)
St Mary Queen Of Martyrs RC Primary School, Hull

The Dream

Dear Diary,

One day I was at my grandma's house and I saw a room so I went inside... I saw a giant golden statue in the centre of the room. Behind it was a long colourful fish tank with hundreds of fish!

When I came out I saw another one. Inside, was empty except for a giant, glowing clock. I walked closer and I realised you could go through it so I did. It was a colourful theme park.

When I was playing on the teacups (like the waltzers) I saw the colour and wonder fading away. I saw a man called Dr Toadstool taking away the wonder with his Won-Taker. I used my locket to get the wonder back and it worked. In the wonderland, everyone was safe.

I went back home to my bedroom and started to read a book.

See ya soon.

Ava Sutherby (9)

St Mary Queen Of Martyrs RC Primary School, Hull

Rebelling

Dear Diary,

Today I was wicked and evil. I put a bucket on top of the classroom door and filled it with cold water! Me and my class were waiting for the teacher. *Swoosh! Splash!* It fell onto my teacher's head, Mrs Green... All of the class was laughing, it was really really funny!

I felt horrid, evil and wicked. It made my day...

After school, my mum was furious. My brother Max was saying, "Ha ha ha, you got in trouble!"

I got really mad. I thought of a plan. My plan was to put a banana skin from my packed lunch from school outside his door. When my mum called for dinner he fell down. It was really funny.

I felt that I was the king of evil. I had no tea that night. I will write soon.

Samuel Oakes (9)
St Mary Queen Of Martyrs RC Primary School, Hull

Jungle Danger

Dear Diary,

I'm called Reece. I am scared of heights and at the moment of going to the jungle. I did and I saw squirrels and I thought I would live.

The bear was nice to me and protected me. A tiger looked like it was going to pounce on me and try to eat me but the bear saved me and battled the tiger to give me more time to run! I lived and the bear too.

Next, I went to a haunted house. There were ghosts trying to get me but I made a machine to make a forcefield so they couldn't catch me or the bear.

Later, the crocodiles in the lake tried to eat me again. I was tired of being animals' food. I found out the rest of the jungle is called Crocodile Island. I wasn't really happy about it.

Reece Wright (9)
St Mary Queen Of Martyrs RC Primary School, Hull

Bad Guy

Dear Diary,

Today a terrible thing happened, my step-sister, Cruella, stole from the rarest jewellery store in London, England. The store is called Barafod. After Cruella stole the diamonds she didn't even get caught because her sneaky boyfriend, Joseph, brought her a grappling gun to grapple herself up to the roof.

After Cruella had robbed the store, she thought to herself, *where am I going to hide all of this, hmmm? I know! I can hide it in my mum's basement.*

The next day, Cruella went back to London to go get some more jewels.

I feel shocked because I have a sis who is a baddie so I said, "I have a sis who is a criminal, wow!"

See you soon.

Sonny Runkee (9)

St Mary Queen Of Martyrs RC Primary School, Hull

The Nightmare Match

Dear Diary,

You won't believe what happened yesterday when I was playing in a football match against West Ham. It was 2-1 to us, I had scored both of the goals, then in the fiftieth minute, I got fouled and had to be taken off the pitch. I ended up at the hospital because I broke my leg. When I was at home resting my leg, watching some TV, eating ice cream with my friend, he said, "Can you walk?" I said, "I'll try." So I tried but then I fell over, so I got back on the couch. The next morning my coach texted me saying: 'Are you coming to training?' I said: 'I can't, my leg is broken'. I will see you soon.

Olly Thompson (9)

St Mary Queen Of Martyrs RC Primary School, Hull

The Brave Leah Williamson

Dear Diary,

You can't believe what she was when she was younger. She was a quiet little girl from England. At school, she wasn't allowed to play football with boys. I would be quite annoyed. As she got older and older she wasn't allowed to play. At home, she was frightened to go to school. She thought *why am I here?*

As she got older and older she got braver and braver. All the nerves went away. She joined a team and the academy of Arsenal U15s. She finally was brave and fought and fought for a place at Arsenal.

Now she is 29 and plays for England and Arsenal and is a captain. She is one of the best.

Will write again soon.

Ava Boyton (9)

St Mary Queen Of Martyrs RC Primary School, Hull

Bory And The Apocalypse

Dear Diary,

You won't believe this... I was going to school and then... Wait, oh yes. Hi, I am Bory. I wear a pan on my head. I'm 13 years old with big eyes.

So let's begin. I was going to school when a portal opened in the sky. Monsters came out. Rad gave me a walkie talkie and we both went home, but my foster family had left me. "Nooo!" I screamed as they drove off.

Then a zombie came after me. I went into my tree house to fix the walkie-talkie and talk to Rad, my friend. We met up to make a cure.

We went to the portal and flung it in and then *boom!* Everything went back to normal.

See you soon!

Bory.

Benjamin Prajsnar (9)

St Mary Queen Of Martyrs RC Primary School, Hull

The Diary Of A Shop Trip

Dear Diary,

Yesterday was the best day of my life! It started off in St Stephens when my mum was in London...

So we were walking in St Stephens and at that point I was tired. Then we walked past a toy shop where my excitement level went from 6 to 10. As soon as I walked in I went to the Nerf section. There was a Nerf ball there. To my surprise, it shot 155 feet. I also got a hand Nerf gun which had two modes - short and long mode.

It turned out that I had some money left so I got mini Among Us characters. I also got a Fart Ninja (disappointing, it broke in 5 mins).

Write again soon,

Edi Mac.

Edward Macpherson (9)

St Mary Queen Of Martyrs RC Primary School, Hull

The Story Of Mohamed Salah

Dear Diary,

I'm Mohamed Salah. I'm from Egypt. I played for Roma then Chelsea and now I play for Liverpool as one of the best in the world.

I retired from Roma then went to Chelsea and now I play for Liverpool.

This all took place in Romania and England. Roma - Romania, London - England and Liverpool - England.

The feeling I've had was I was upset when I lost the Champions League and the Prem.

Some other ideas are that I assisted Roberto Firmino's last Anfield goal and Roberto Firmino assisted my first Anfield goal.

Bye for now

Mohamed Salah.

Jacob Smalley (9)
St Mary Queen Of Martyrs RC Primary School, Hull

The Minion

Dear Diary,

Something happened to me. I was going to my secret base in the basement and when I went in my basement was tidy. So I did my experiment.

Bang!

"Who is at the door?" I said.

No one was there so I stared. I accidentally dropped it and the chemicals. I screamed because it was a monster. It was a Minion.

I hope I see you again.

Bye for now.

Mercy-Rae Robinson (9)

St Mary Queen Of Martyrs RC Primary School, Hull

Park

Dear Diary,

You won't believe this. I was walking for fresh air and a *woosh!* I got pooped on! Disgusting animal, yuck! I was cleaning it but it's not coming out. Bye for now.

Kaiden Howard (9)

St Mary Queen Of Martyrs RC Primary School, Hull

Diary Of An Amazing Kid

Dear Diary,

My name is Leo Ralphail Beilzzubub the Third and in this world, people are born at one million like how you were born at one. I have a dog named Bennimaru but we call him Beni. He is 1,000 years old. I have a little sis and she is 6 million years old. Her name is Chara, she has a twin who is a boy and named Sans. I almost forgot about my age. I am 69 million and we get superpowers at the age of 50 million. We age faster too. But enough about introductions, time for action. You know how I said we get superpowers I still don't have mine and my dad said I was just a late bloomer but I don't think so, it's been 19 million years so I don't know why it hasn't happened. Later I felt something ominous about myself. Beni started barking at me which was weird until I looked at my arm and saw blue flames! Later I learned how to control it and soon it was mine and I was using it. I was saved by my dad. The twins were standing right next to Dad and they had a huge smile across their faces. It made me smile too but the day was coming to an end so at last I shot fire to the sky which made fireworks. Tomorrow I will see another day.

Eric Udo-Uzoagba (10)
St Richard's RC Primary School, Atherton

Diary Of A Superhero

An extract

Dear Diary,

Today has been a crazy day. Let me start from the beginning. I woke up in the morning, had my crunchy nibbles and then I went to lick Racheal's face because you can't lick your owner's face without having breakfast first. How rude of me, I haven't told you my name yet. Anyways, my name is Rex and my superhero name is Wonder Dog, yes you heard me right, I am secretly a superhero but don't tell anyone. Now you must be wondering how I am able to write, right? Well, I am a special superhero and I have the power to create any superpower I want so right now I am levitating a pencil.

Now back to my day, I finished licking her face and went to sleep on my navy blue bed again but just as I was getting comfy my collar started beeping, which meant someone was causing trouble. I quickly transformed into Wonder Dog and went to the location given by my collar. Soon I would find how much harder this mission would be than the rest.

Once I got there Emperor Cat was waiting for me. "Wonder Dog, what a nice surprise!" giggled Emperor Cat.

"Emperor Cat, I should have known," I barked back.

You must also be asking how all the other missions I have had were so easy. Well, I created a little something called a power bark. It's a normal bark but a lot louder so I just blew my enemies away...

Erica Udo-Uzoagba (10)

St Richard's RC Primary School, Atherton

The Diary Of A Lost Twin

An extract

Dear Diary,

When I woke up I was so excited because today was my birthday. I looked through the window to check if Orchid and her mum were there. To my surprise, I saw a van. It said 'Pets At Home'. My mum told me to close my eyes and come away from the window, that's how I knew it was for me. When the door opened I heard a barking sound. My mum told me to close my eyes because I was peeking but I couldn't hold my curiosity. I sat on the couch and felt someone lickling my face.

I opened my eyes and saw that it was a dog. I started to cry happy tears and as I looked around the room something caught my eye, tickets. Orchid came through the door and screamed, "We're going to LA." It was like a dream come true, first a dog and then tickets to LA. What else? Money raining through the sky? I panicked because I hadn't packed my bags but Mum stood there with a suitcase in her hand with my name on it. I ran to Mum and Orchid and gave them a bear hug.

On the back of the tickets, there was some more. There were tickets to watch Lady Gaga and I decided the name for my dog, Gaga.

I heard a honk outside and it was an Uber. Orchid's mum was already in it. I thanked all my family and friends and we rushed to the car...

Abisola Ilupeju (10)
St Richard's RC Primary School, Atherton

Invaders

Dear Diary,

Today was very strange! I went through a crazy magical adventure. The day started pretty normally. I was outside with my sister. She was reading a book as I slowly wandered off. I was turning around when I noticed something strange, a hole. It looked like it had been there for years untouched. As I looked in I couldn't see the end. As I came closer I noticed the grass around it had changed colour into a greyish colour. As I looked in I wasn't able to hold my grip and fell in. As I came closer to a strange thing that looked like grass but I was certain it wasn't grass I noticed my gravity started to change, it was like I was swimming but in air. Once I landed on the strange substance it was soft and very dark. I looked up but it was like the hole disappeared into thin air. I didn't have enough time to breathe before I heard something. I quickly hid behind something that resembled a tree but it was metal. As the sound got louder I saw something strange. A robot. It looked old and like a single poke could break it. Its eyes were green with a side of blue.

As it looked around its eyes changed to bloodlust red. I didn't dare flinch, not even a breath. It luckily passed by but whatever it was I didn't trust it...

Alex Malaj (10)

St Richard's RC Primary School, Atherton

My Trip To Greece

Dear Diary,

I went to Greece with my family in the summer. I went to visit the Colosseum and when we got there, there was a bull running around freely. Since it was summer, it was really hot. We went to the waterpark back at the hotel; the water was really cold and it felt the best! After that, I got an alert saying it was a moderate thunderstorm! Luckily it was the day that we went home. I was really excited to see Lily, Serena, Lucie, Gracie, Lexi and Katy until we found out our flight was cancelled! Summer and Katie were kind of sad and happy because they both exclaimed, "More tanning!" Evie-Rose and I had mixed emotions but it meant more swimming! We went back to the hotel and told them we wanted to book back in. The receptionist said that somebody had already claimed the room. My mum was furious until the receptionist said that there were two rooms free. One room had one bed and the other one had two beds. We claimed them both. Luckily, they had a door to connect them together.

As soon as we got there Mum got a phone call saying the flight was back up and was ready to board but Mum said, "No," and put the phone down on the bed.

Lily King (10)
St Richard's RC Primary School, Atherton

Freddie The Dog

Dear Diary,

Today was the best day ever, I woke up and got changed into some clothes like usual. It was a very sunny day so I needed to go outside. We did not know where to go so we did a vote. We chose ice cream. I got into the car and drove to the ice cream parlour, it was so yummy. We were driving back when we drove past a dog rescue home and as my sister loves dogs we decided to have a look at them. We were not going to buy a dog until all we could hear was dogs barking apart from one. That was Freddie the sausage dog. As we were going to leave my sister ran to Freddie and picked him up. She would not move away from him so we had no choice but to buy him.

We went into the office to ask the man if we could buy him. He said, "Of course, he's the best dog." The man kindly introduced us to Freddie and even let us give him a treat! At this point, we all fell in love with Freddie so we signed the contract and took him home! We did not have any dog supplies so we took him to the pet shop.

We even made him a special nametag. We all love Freddie very much and are going to make some great memories with him. We will see what tomorrow brings.

Serena Price (10)

St Richard's RC Primary School, Atherton

Today I Watched A Movie

Dear Diary,

Today I was at home, I opened the TV and started to watch a movie. My mum asked me to do my homework but I was so tired I didn't want to, I wanted to watch my movie. Mum said, "If you finish your homework you can watch the movie!" I said, "Okay, Mum," and started to do my homework. "Mum, I've finished my homework, can I watch the movie now?" I said.

"No, because it is lunchtime!" she said.

"Okay," I said.

When I finished my lunch I asked, "Mum, can I watch the movie?"

"Yes you can," she said.

One hour later, Mum said, "You need to stop watching the movie and read a book!"

"Okay," I said to reading the book.

After two minutes I said, "I've finished reading, can I watch the movie?"

"Yes, but you can only watch it for thirty minutes."

"Okay."

Thirty minutes later Mum said, "You need to read a book."

I said, "Mum, I need to go to sleep."
"Okay, goodnight."
"Goodnight Mum," I said.

Abigail Ip (10)

St Richard's RC Primary School, Atherton

Mia's Holiday

Dear Diary,

It was a good day today, the best day ever. I went on holiday. I went to see my family in Wales. I thought we were staying for two weeks but it turned out to be three weeks instead. We got to the beach at 2pm so we could enjoy the big bright blue waves. Suddenly I found a kitten. I thought to myself, *should I keep her or try to find her owner? I think I should tell my uncle Luke because he knows everyone in Wales so obviously he should know who she is.* Uncle Luke said she was his cat but I could have her so I named her Lila. I thought it was a beautiful name to give this five-month-old kitten. Suddenly, Lila bit me in my uncle's back garden. I was so upset that I cried with tears. I wonder what is going to happen tomorrow...

Mia-Jayed Richards (10)

St Richard's RC Primary School, Atherton

The Missing Dog

Dear Diary,

Today is a special day for me. It's my birthday. I am a Staffy and I'm turning two today. I'm so happy. I got so many presents. My mum went to put something in the bin and left the front door open so I snuck outside and ran out. In a flash, I was lost but I wasn't scared. I was really tired so I had a little nap and when I woke up I ran and ran. I found a really cool park, it wasn't that colourful, I could only see blue and yellow. I had so much fun at the park. I left the park and ran and ran until I saw a big huge palace. There were five guards near the gates but I found a hole and I went through it. I saw the king, he was so amazing and he adopted me. I will write to you again tomorrow.

Lucie Sumner (10)

St Richard's RC Primary School, Atherton

The Day I Was Bitten By My Friend

Dear Diary,

Today has been a weird but exciting day. I got a call on my pizza box, it was from Batman asking if I wanted to go to the waterpark with him. I packed my towel, swimming costume, goggles and suncream just in case the outside pool was open. At the waterpark, Batman paid for us. We went on all the new and old slides. We went outside and I sat down. I suggested going to get something to eat but just as we were finishing someone bit me. See you tomorrow, diary.

Ruby Cunliffe (9)

St Richard's RC Primary School, Atherton

The Robbery Of The Pizza Shop

Dear Diary,

Today was insane, let me go back. I was walking around the shop until a robber broke in and tried to eat me. Nobody was in so I had to defend myself. I threw fruit at the robber but he wouldn't stop sprinting after me. When I ran into my best friend, Dino, he ate up the robber.

Freddie (10)

St Richard's RC Primary School, Atherton

The Little Bomb

Dear Diary,

It's already been a war for a few months. The war between America and Japan still continues. But that's not happened today, although Japan lost most of their force, however, they didn't give up, not till today!

That gave the only way to do it. The American government wanted the Air Force to launch the powerful little bomb, the strongest bomb in the world. It probably can turn one and a half cities into flat land. So I took the bomb to Tokyo. This bomb, not even Russia could make it. Although it could launch on a plan, but it was still not easy because Japan was not 100% destroyed. Luckily, the F-117 could handle Japan's force. So I could launch the little bomb easily.

When the smog was over I could see the damage that I had done. I was thinking, *I launched the little bomb. It was a little action but already made a huge history. All the buildings and wildlife that I have destroyed.* I watched the destroyed Tokyo until I couldn't see the land.

Nathan Chow (10)

St Thomas The Martyr CE Primary School & Nursery, Up Holland

Diary Of Detective Ed

Dear Diary,

I'm shocked, scared, angry and determined. I don't even know what to feel. My best friend was murdered! She knew it would happen sooner or later as there was a weird criminal stalker in her apartment and as the lead detective of England's society, I was invited to the crime scene. You won't believe what happened when I arrived!

When I made it to the crime scene all I could see was drops of blood and a note. I picked it up and drawn in red ink was a picture of me. On the floor. Dead. I read the writing. It had two words: 'You're next'. I didn't recognise the scrawly handwriting but I did recognise that something or someone was now coming for me too...

Emily Dean (11)

St Thomas The Martyr CE Primary School & Nursery, Up Holland

Changing Views

An extract

Dear Diary,

I was so angry! Why did no one like black people? We are the same as white! And even the police... of all people, they should be the people stopping this not starting it!

I calmed myself and decided to go somewhere to shop. I bought all the things I needed and went to the counter.

The man calculated the price and said, "You look like you've had a rough day. What happened?"

I knew I could trust him, my mum said so.

"Stupid police officers," I mumbled.

"What did they do?"

I told my story yet again and in the end, he said, "I used to be a police officer for ten years. I was the chief of police, in fact. One day someone planted drugs in my pocket. I got fired on the spot."

"I'm sorry!" I gasped.

"You don't need to be."

"No, I shou- Wait, do you think you can help me? No one will listen to me because I'm black."

"Umm..."

"Please?" I begged.

"Fine, I'll try. But I'm not going to speak to the police officers, I'm just going to tell you what to say," he said and told me what to do.

A minute later, I strode into the supermarket. I was ready to speak. It took me a while to get their attention but standing on the counter worked.

"Nearly everyone thinks black people are different and unique but we all are. We are different and ourselves. Instead of teasing each other for that, as the police do," the police officers looked sheepishly at their feet, "we need to respect each other."

Even if I didn't change the world, I had changed the police officer's point of view. And that's a small win!

Ellie Plumpton (10)
Stillness Junior School, London

The Disastrous Diary Of A Super Nerdy Teen

Dear Diary,

I have a confession to make! I know this might, and most likely will, send your brain flying full way around the universe and then back again!

Okay, breathe. I accidentally killed my mum's favourite orange tree! Phew, glad that's out. Anyway, enough of this little girlie chit-chat, let me tell you how this awful event played out...

Well, Mum was away on this mega boring business trip so I was left alone in a big house, in charge of everything, everything! 1. Feeding Tiddles (the cat). 2. Taking out the bins. 3. Washing Mum's bras and pants. It's ridiculous. She treats me as if I am a common housemaid in a posh Victorian household. Mum had been gone for seven days and everything was going just fine (although I did dye her knickers orange when I left my pants in the wash). Until I realised... I hadn't watered Mum's plants! How could I forget something so important?! Mum would be so angry. I was meant to water them once a day! And I hadn't so much as glanced in their direction.

Without delay, I rushed downstairs, spilling water all over the floor, from the watering can that I'd filled up, as I ran to the conservatory!

Then I heard it, that sound that sent a shiver down my spine. The key turned in the lock with a sudden... click. Oh, no, she was here!

I ran upstairs at lightning speed. I rushed into my room and locked the door.

I'm writing this from the safety of my room. I've just finished the sentence and I can hear her coming up the stairs... Please... what do I do?! Help!

Kitty Chambers (10)
Stillness Junior School, London

What A Nightmare

An extract

Dear Diary,

Breathtaking! That is the only word I can think of to describe what happened yesterday. Last night, Dad announced that me and my sister were going to Disneyland in Paris. I was overjoyed!

Mum told me that it would be better if I packed the suitcases early - probably linking back to last year when we ran a whole six hours late for our trip! Dad couldn't find his toothbrush (which is totally normal for him).

Anyway, I went to bed that night, pondering if any bad things would occur during our holiday but I decided to not think about it much and fell fast asleep.

Before I knew it, the day ahead arrived. Whilst my alarm clock screamed its lungs out, I leapt out of bed and gleefully brushed my teeth as excited jazz music randomly started playing in my head; the smell of breakfast had already reached my nose. As fast as a cheetah, I zoomed across the house, somersaulted into the living room and sprang onto the dinner table.

As I walked through the railway station I only had one thing in my mind: Disneyland. But what I didn't know was that everything would start to drastically change.

As we were walking through the station the speaker started to say something. "Attention, please, all trains have been cancelled."

At that moment, I was heartbroken and I was just about to burst into tears until...

Snap! I woke up in a cold sweat. I looked around in confusion and utter shock. It was all just a dream! I was happy and relieved. The trip isn't even until next week!

Ryan Tin (10)
Stillness Junior School, London

Books, Books And Devils

An extract

Dear Diary,

Today has been a sad, scary, horrifying day. I was getting ready to go to school. I knew there was no point saying bye as both my parents were fighting so I grabbed an apple and went to school.

When I got home I found my mum sitting at the kitchen table with black wet bags of make-up around her eyes, with a piece of paper in front of her reading 'Divorce paper'. Tears filled my eyes. I couldn't take it anymore. I ran to my den - my den is a place in the park that only I know.

Once I was ready to go back home I made a slow stroll back. I noticed that a boy (who looked around the age of fifteen) had been taking the same route as me. I assumed he lived in the same area as me, but by the time I had reached my house, he was standing right by the door like it was nothing. I knew something was up. I couldn't tell my mum (there was just too much on her plate) and I had no clue where my dad was so I guess it was up to me.

I packed my bag and when the boy left I followed him. He was pretty fast so I couldn't see him when he turned the corner, but when I did there was nothing there but a bookshop called Dimensional Books. Suddenly I felt a small sense of eagerness to go in the shop. So I did.

In there, I found a book called The Devil's Child. It looked interesting so I started to feel something as if I was getting sucked into a... book...!

Kyla Lennon (10)

Stillness Junior School, London

Bad Luck

An extract

Dear Diary,

The past few weeks have been quite rough for me. In case you're new here, I am Hazle. As I was saying, last week the whole of my street's lights went down which for me is a problem big enough to fit a space shuttle into.

My whole life is gone but luckily I still have my best friend, Amy. When we hang out together it's normally because we have some kind of basketball thing on later. When we are together we normally make slime or watch a movie.

It's heartbreaking because in two days Amy is moving permanently to Spain. I am ashamed to admit this but I am quite lazy. One of my biggest problems is that if Amy moves to Spain then I have to do my own homework and buy my own carrier. I am trying to learn how to write like Amy so that my homework is believable. All this is going to be a big adjustment to my life so I hope it doesn't end badly.

If you did not know then I am about to move to secondary and my parents are pleading to get me into a private school which sucks.

Last night, I came downstairs to watch a horror movie with my friend when my brother Timmy came down and because he is only three years old I got told off. Once Mum saw what was on she turned on Teletubbies which is so unfair because it was four hours after his bedtime.

Rowena Streatfeild (9)
Stillness Junior School, London

My Disastrous Half Term

An extract

Dear Diary,

Oh my goodness! That is probably the only way to start this. This was near lunch on a hot, sunny day and my younger brother, whose name is Timmy, was jumping up and over the waves that were crashing onto the sand. Meanwhile, my very little sister called Lilly was making sand angels (and putting bows on them as usual). Anyway, I barely do as I'm told so I got my swimming costume on and ran in!

On the way in my mum was saying, "Not too deep, there is no lifeguard on this beach."

I didn't listen again and a few minutes later I couldn't touch the floor anymore. Then out of nowhere, a long fin came out of the water! I laughed happily! *What!* I thought it was a dolphin. But then it opened its mouth and... darkness! I had been eaten by a shark! I could tell because I was in its throat and the teeth definitely gave it away! Amazingly, I spotted the gross pink gills and I could see out of them! I saw we were in a giant fish tank.

I brushed past the bones of all the different animals, holding my breath and then I realised exactly where I was... I was in the underwater aquarium full of sharks!

Isobel Minns (10)
Stillness Junior School, London

The Big Search

23/2/2011

Dear Diary,

Can you believe that someone has gone missing in our very own village? Everybody has their own theories - some think aliens, others suspect the mafia but I know what really happened. There is something lurking in the forest and believe me, I'm going to find out what.

24/2/2011

Dear Diary,

Today I arrived five minutes late to school due to a new route I followed to avoid going near the forest. Everyone disagrees with me. They say, "It was clearly just a mistake, they must have moved out." But no, I know it was the forest. I just need to prove it. I'll send my mum to check it out. She will come back tomorrow. And if she doesn't I'll look for her.

25/2/2011

Dear Diary,

I couldn't take it anymore! I have to look for her. I've brought my torch, this diary and a packed dinner - well, hopefully, I'll be back for dinner.

I'm at the forest now, just writing this last part before I venture in and then (fingers crossed) write the rest when I come back.

Oh no! I hear something coming! Hopefully, I'll write more tomorrow...

Gregor Jackman (10)

Stillness Junior School, London

A Refugee Kid's Diary

Dear Diary,

My legs are aching horribly and I've already walked for about two miles. Why another? I'm just a refugee kid.

Sorry, I didn't write yesterday. It was because of the bomb. Yesterday I woke up to a bomb. It was loud, so loud my house actually shook! You may be thinking, *yay! That sounds so fun* but it's not, it's more like a massive roller coaster that makes you feel sick, dizzy and sad.

At school, I once learnt about war and now I'm suffering from it. I had to grab all I could but it was all blurry then from my salty tears. Then I had to run, leaving Daddy behind. I hope he'll be okay.

I wish war wasn't like this. And to think I'm just one little girl called Layla Sennit. There are a lot of people struggling out there.

Write soon! Bye Diary. See ya! XOX.

Beatrice Roebuck (9)

Stillness Junior School, London

The Fantasy Fish

Dear Diary,

Guess what? This morning, I went swimming in the freezing azure sea, and I met and greeted an enchanting rose-pink and ruby fish with sparkly, shiny scales. When I first laid my eyes on it, I thought they were playing cheeky tricks on my brain, but to prove whether it was real or not, I swiftly swam up to it. *It was real!* It told me, in a soft, princess-like voice, that it could tell the future. "Tonight, you will have vegetable lasagne with mashed potato - your absolute number-one dinner!"

I gaped at it. My bottom jaw refused to go back up. How did this random little fish know what I was having for dinner? I stared at the miniature lilac stars coming out from the fish's body, through my tight, painful goggles. The disgustingly salty water hurt my throat, so I shut my mouth. I waved goodbye to it, but in the blink of an eye, it disappeared, leaving tiny sparkles behind.

When I was lying in bed after lunch, I wondered what else is out there on Earth that hasn't been discovered...

Reet Gandhi (9)
The Stoke Poges School, Stoke Poges

(A Bit Of A) Dance Disaster!

Dear Diary,

Aaah, oh em gee! Worst day *ever*. Today is the day my lifelong dream of performing in *Las Vegas* comes true! I'm performing with my super friendly BFFs in these super chic dresses. Oh, wait, where's my one? *In pieces!* Like my heart. I can't let my BFFs down, it's not only *my dream* but theirs too! It all started when I looked at my desk when I opened my new room for the week - oh my! It had a lavender-scented sheet, beautiful! My BFFs were next to my room. Guess who was opposite me... my *super-rude-and-annoying* frenemy, Jessica! So unfair, like, my life *literally* depends on this! *Ugh.* Anyway, I remember putting my *super chic* dress directly on my bed! So, who could it be? *Obviously Jessica* (she hates my guts!) To be honest, I hate her guts *too!* Back to the present day, I texted my BFFs and called an ECBSBH (Emergency Chat Because Something Bad Happened!).

We went over who could've been the dress assassin - the only person we realised could have done it was *little Miss Dress Killer Jessica!* Amellie was all like - "Let's confront her!" But Sehaj said that we should confront her *gently...* I agreed with Sehaj, but on the inside, I went for Amellie's idea!

So, we went to fix my dress.
#Regret-Saying-My-Dress-Is-In-Pieces! *Eeeek!* My dress is, like, so *pretty!* I could have a heart attack! So, I had the idea to rub my outfit in Jess' face (not literally!).
Wish me luck, XOXO.

Alice Weaver (9)
The Stoke Poges School, Stoke Poges

Ronaldo's First Football Match

Dear Diary,

I wake up. I'm about to get ready for a football club. I eat breakfast, I get dressed and I go.

I've finished my match at the football club. I'm about to leave when the coach calls me. "What is it, coach?"

He says, "Pack your bags 'cause you're going to a stadium!"

"What?!" I say. "When?"

"Tomorrow."

"Huh," I say. I can't believe I just volunteered to play football against Argentina. I'm only seventeen! What are my friends gonna say? I mean, me?! Cristiano Ronaldo - me?! I asked my coach, "How do they know me?"

He says, "I sent them a video of you playing football and asked them how good you were, and they said, "Ooh," so now you're their captain."

"Huh?!" I say. "I'm ready!" I say.

I've got the ball. I aim, I shoot and I... miss. I put all my strength and confidence into the shot, but then I noticed it wasn't a miss, it was a save. So, it bounces back, I shoot and... I score!

Sui! I get three more goals, Bruno gets two more goals. Rui Patricio saved and we won! 6-nil! 6-0! We won!

Gabriel Carmo (9)

The Stoke Poges School, Stoke Poges

The End Of The Rainbow

Dear Diary,

Last night, I was in my small London office when the phone rang. I know it was my day off but, as a detective, my curiosity got the better of me, so, without hesitation, I answered the phone. It was a strange voice, the sort that you wouldn't have heard of before. I gasped in shock! They had spoken of the end of the rainbow. This was an astonishing discovery, so I asked for the address and set off with my partner, Agether Hood. After what felt like a year of meandering through the forest, we came across a pair of bedazzling golden gates. No one knew the forest better than I did, but I had never seen them before. My brain began to make fizzing noises. I opened the gate, hoping for the best, but all that was there was another gate. In confusion, I opened that one too. If I had not answered that phone call, I would never have experienced such a bedazzling sight. Paradise, it was a land of pure paradise. There was the end of the rainbow too! Its rainbow colours shone over the lush green grass and peaceful animals.

Pots of gold in every corner.
Yours sincerely,
Clara Hayles.

Madeleine Briggs (9)
The Stoke Poges School, Stoke Poges

Kylo Ren's Diary

Dear Diary,

Today, I woke up on the Star Destroyer while we were attacking the Resistance Armada. I got ready into my suit, got my lightsabre, went in my supreme panel ship, put my lightsabre next to me and attacked the Millennium Falcon. Suddenly, we had to retreat because the Resistance called reinforcements, so I landed back in the Star Destroyer and we went to Starkiller Base (our base). After we got there, I went to the prison cells, killed ninety-nine of them and questioned one. He said he wouldn't say anything, so I threatened him so he said they were regrouping in Nabor. So, we set off to Nabor and, fortunately, they were there, so we exploded the Millenium Falcon. We then switched the landing button so we went on solid ground. My troops went attacking and then I got my lightsabre and turned it on. Luke Skywalker echoed by doing the same. We then bashed our lightsabres together. We had to retreat because we were outnumbered and I think a bang on the head took my memory away...

Kairon Arya (9)
The Stoke Poges School, Stoke Poges

The Incredible Diary Of Harrison

Dear Diary,

Today was the craziest day of my life! So, first, there was an assembly at school to annoy me. The whole school was going to *Lego Land*. Each class got their own minibus and we drove off to Lego Land. It all started out like a normal, boring school trip, so me and my sister snuck off. We wandered around for a while (we got lost at one point!). Finally, we found the swimming centre, but then I realised I had left my swimming trunks in the locker room. I didn't want to go back to the locker room but I really wanted to go swimming, so I ran back, grabbed my trunks, my diary and a pencil. I changed into my trunks and ran to the swimming pool. We jumped in and swam around for a while, but then everything went black...

I had got sucked into a black hole! It was very scary and then I fell, I landed on something hard. I was in real-life Lego Land! Everything was made out of Lego, *even me!* And I'm still stuck here now!

Josephine Donnelly (9)

The Stoke Poges School, Stoke Poges

Megalodon Misfit

Dear Diary,

I am all lonely. I've... I've eaten all my friends. What else was I supposed to eat? I'm starving and really I can't see anything because there is nothing more dark than the black, deep, dark society (the bottom of the ocean). As you know, my name is 'helpless' Zareeda, the last Megalodon in the world. It sounds all cool, yeah, but it's not at all. I literally only have one tooth. I wish I'd be back with Papa Megeralin and Mama Merinda. Only Mama's special algae recipe would make my teeth grow back. I mean, I am only forty-three (*sigh*). *I just want to be normal!* Sorry, Diary, it's just I've already meditated eleven times.

Well, I best be off then, as 'an extinct species'. You should really teach me how to properly meditate. Anyway, I might try to catch some food.

Bye, my humanly book.

Zara Dar (9)

The Stoke Poges School, Stoke Poges

Lost As Lego

Dear Diary,

Today, started normal but then got crazy. I was on the plane to Florida; normal, getting called a geek, I was with my friends, Josephine and Olivia. I could just about hear Max screaming. Max is my brother's friend. It was already 8pm. We left school at 12pm. I had already eaten, but I was still hungry. I felt my big, plump tummy - maybe Mum was right - I needed to stop eating so much. I fell asleep...

The next day, I woke up and everybody was going out of the plane. I grabbed my stuff and took Josephine's hand. Olivia grabbed Josephine's hand. We went out and we got on a bus. About ten minutes later, we got off. I saw my brother, he saw me, he came running.

"Let's go swimming!" he said.

I said, "Okay..."

We went to the pool, I jumped in, I was Lego...

From Lilly May.

Lucy Chapman (9)
The Stoke Poges School, Stoke Poges

Lost

Dear Diary,

As I walked through the damp, dark and gloomy forest, blood-red eyes peered through the thorny bushes. My heart leapt and my body grew stiff. I deeply regret running away now.

I felt like I was being followed, an icy chill ran down my spine. As the thunder roared and the lightning raved, a sudden storm broke out. Cold, wet splatters drenched me from head to toe. I had to go, I had to leave!

Suddenly, an eerie archway appeared before me. Ivy crawled up the arch. The arch was made of a pearly white slab of polished grey stone. As the fog rolled in, I started to sink into the icky mud. My heart leapt; was it really the end?

The next thing I knew, I heard a soft, gentle voice. "Wake up."

I woke up with bright lights shining.

"Hello? Where am I?" I cried to the woman...

Anika Mandokhot (9)

The Stoke Poges School, Stoke Poges

The Wild Child

Dear Diary,

Something terrible happened a few days ago. I went on holiday to South Africa. As we got off the plane, I saw bloodthirsty-looking animals staring into my soul. I stumbled across the airport, just to look for the exit with my parents. We finally reached the exit. Terrified, I lay my head on my mum's shoulder. As we walked out, I felt shivers down my spine. The tingling sensation made me uncomfortable. My parents were unpacking, so I had to go feed the wild animals when, all of a sudden, *a cheetah pounced on me!* I got knocked out...

As soon as I woke up, *I had shrunk!* I was as tiny as an ant and I was stuck on a cobweb. Just before I could look away, a *rhino* walked into the cobweb! I was scared to death. As the rhino was trying to lick the cobweb, I got *eaten! Aah!*

Mia Lee (9)

The Stoke Poges School, Stoke Poges

The Director's Death

Dear Diary,

Today, one of the scariest things happened! We were filming for the movie and then I found the director in my dressing room, dead! Who could have killed him? It might be his ex-girlfriend, Mary, who wants to get revenge; or his wife, Elizabeth, who is always complaining that he is too lazy. So, I looked at the evidence and I found a red lipstick! Mary wears pink lipstick, so it was Elizabeth! I went and confronted her and she said, "Yes, I did it." So, I called the cops and she got arrested. I was so happy, we called the CEO director and said, "You are the new director, Mark." He was so excited! Filming the film was so fun and I watched it last night for movie night. It was so good.
Millie Bobby Brown.

Amellie Barrett-Allchin (9)
The Stoke Poges School, Stoke Poges

The Lost Golden Orb

Once, in London, there was a huge famous museum that had antiques and all sorts of different antiques. Everybody knew that there was a room with the golden orb and the code '2014'. One night, a mysterious thief came into the museum and he knew the code. He did it, he stole the golden orb and left a note saying 'I have stolen the orb, try and find me'. The next day, the boss of the museum checked the room with the orb because it was open. Oh no!

"The orb is gone, call our detective."

So, they did and outside was a trail of footprints. She followed them and she found the thief, and Kacy called the police and he got arrested. Kacy Berrel got a job to be an actual detective.

Khadija Ali (8)

The Stoke Poges School, Stoke Poges

The Jungle Boy

Dear Diary,

I was flying to New Zealand on the plane, the co-pilot announced, "Put your seatbelts on." So, everyone put their seatbelts on. All of a sudden, we were *going down!* There was a big crash! After that, I didn't know where I was. Then I knew I was in the jungle (sounds like an adventure). At first, I was like, "Oh my god!" Then I was like, "YAY! I can have loads of fun." So, first I got sticks, vines and leaves and made a den out of them. I went to get berries but when I came back there was a chopper. It said: 'Safety helicopter'. They came to rescue me, but I was annoyed about it and now here I am - at my hotel in New Zealand!

Veer Benawra (9)

The Stoke Poges School, Stoke Poges

Ancient Time

Dear Diary,

You will *never* believe what happened yesterday. So, you see, I was just going up the slippery steps of my school with Kristy (my absolute best friend) when... an *alarm* went off. There was smoke everywhere! Suddenly, a green, swirling black hole sucked me rapidly, out of nowhere. I screamed with terror, Diary. I mean, me, who everyone calls brave non-sarcastically. Anyway, *the portal sucked me in* and now I'm going to go and follow a random ancient Egyptian person! Why am I living in ancient times?!

Hafsah Malik (9)

The Stoke Poges School, Stoke Poges

The Camping Trip

Dear Diary,

I went camping with my family. I was so excited to go there. As we got there, we had to get everything out of the car and put them in the hut.

Day two

After I had finished breakfast, we went fishing. I didn't catch any fish yet. After finishing, we had chicken for lunch and dinner, then I went to bed.

Day three

It was the last day of camping and I went back home, then I had a haircut and I went in a hot tub.

Finn McGarvey (8)

The Stoke Poges School, Stoke Poges

The World Cup Final

Dear Diary,

It started on the bus. I was talking to Jofra Archer. We were playing New Zealand it was going to be a hard match. Jofra bowled and he got a wicket. They ended at 256. We battled and I hit 150, but then I got out. Jofra scored a lot and it was very stressful. It ended with 256 runs because of a no-ball. We hit it for 6, so we went into a super-over. We batted first, and I went in with Jos Buttler. We scored 15 and New Zealand got 15, and it was down to Jofra Archer, and we both ended on 15. It went down to a boundary count and we knew it because of the last ball. They got a run and we knew we'd won so we all ran and celebrated a very scary win. We spent the next hour celebrating and it was so much fun, I got to talk to the commentators and I was so happy we won. All of the New Zealand team was crying, so I went over there and comforted them and I eventually got in the changing room and then we went on the bus. That was the end of a manic day.

Elliot Shelley (10)
Yarlet School, Yarlet

A Reality Mess

Dear Diary,

Yesterday was the weirdest, greatest and scariest day in my whole life! I don't know how I'm going to explain it, but I'll give it my best shot!

It was a normal morning, I had my shower, got dressed and had my breakfast. I hopped into my car and hit the road for work. I lived in a very quiet country area, but I loved it! Having a big, peaceful garden really boosts my mood! Anyway, as I was driving to work, I saw a weird portal thing on the edge of the road. I parked my car and walked on foot to this mysterious thing, intrigued and excited. I touched the swirling, glowing portal and I was gone. I completely disappeared from Earth!

I opened my eyes and I was in a different reality! It was a weird place, a dark, dull, black world filled with broken and destroyed buildings. Just as I decided to move forward and explore, a big creature popped out from behind a building and started to chase me! I ran as fast as I could, dodging poisonous puddles on the ground, but the creature was gaining on me. I was petrified! When he was around five yards behind me, he lifted his massive, burnt, grey and deathly hand and slashed at me...

Everything went black. All of a sudden, I felt really warm and could feel my body. My eyes opened and I was in my warm, cosy bed. It was all a dream.

Bertie Shammas (10)
Yarlet School, Yarlet

The Mission!

Dear Diary,

Today, I was given a mission. A mysterious mission, a mission I wasn't expecting, a mission to defeat the Fungi king! Us mushrooms have been at war with the Fungis! But, to be the one to end this would be historical! I would be a hero! So, I started by packing my walnut slingshot and hopping into the Mushy Mobile! The Mushy Mobile is covered in mushroom patterns with...

Anyway, as I started my journey, I stumbled across a swamp, a swamp with a sign saying *No Mushrooms.* So, I suddenly got concerned! The terrain wasn't flat, so I couldn't use the Mushy Mobile. So, I went on foot, step by step. It started to feel like I was walking in circles! But, just before I quit, I saw the Fungi kingdom, so I entered! I snuck behind the guards, I crept up the stairs and I could see him! With one deep breath, I pulled the slingshot out of my pocket, I placed a poisonous pebble in the patch and *bang*, the Fungi king was destroyed with one hit. "*Bullseye!*" That was the first word I said before disaster...

The worst thing happened... Just kidding! You really thought?!

Anyway, that is how I completed the mission.

Mushroom.

Harry Cookson-Jones (11)

Yarlet School, Yarlet

The Diary Of The Mean One!

Dear Diary,

Do you want to know the first person I see when I walk into school? Her, of course, but this time she has short hair, so I walk up to her and ask why she got it and she says, "For a change." But, like, that isn't an answer. Then I realised, I told her she looked like a Karen and she stayed still while I walked over to my other friends, and she went to her 'friend' when she was supposed to be following me and just listening to me and not interrupt me

A few minutes later, the whistle blew and, of course, that girl was frowning. What an attention-seeker. As we line up, I see my boyfriend arrive. We call him over.

"Hi, Chico."

For registration, me and Chico are talking and what do I know? She is talking to her 'friend'. I'm not trying to sound jealous, but he's my ex! I stare at her, she's laughing. I ask her why she spent eight years of being *my* BFF for nothing!

Cora Norris (11)

Yarlet School, Yarlet

The Sock

Dear Diary,

Horrible, just horrible. Today, my human decided to buy a new sock, even though he knows I hate wonderful smells. Roger (my human) specifically said, "Ooh, my feet smell, especially Big Bad Daddy Toe!" in a girly voice. I don't even know if he knows I (Big Bad Daddy Toe, they call me BBD Toe for short) exist. So, Roger decided to get a new sock, which is bad for me so that's bad for him. We were on our way to the sock shop and he/we bumped into a girl who was so stinky, I reckon she could be Big Bad Mummy Toe, oh wahoo! After we got to the shops, we were on our way to Sock Shop whilst thinking about the future (BBMT). Oh no, I wasn't meant to put that in... Okay, so we got to the shop and there it was, a spectacularly smelly-not sock and, suddenly, the shopkeeper got it out and gave it to Roger. Roger opened it and...

"*Aaaaah, Mummy!*"

Logan Kerr (11)
Yarlet School, Yarlet

Post, Post, Crossbar

Dear Diary,

Today was controversial. I woke up and was in my blacked-out shed at Anfield, and I was talking to Right Post. Crossbar was still sleeping, as usual. Every time the ball hits him, he shakes and rattles. Anyway, today was game day. Liverpool vs Southampton. The groundsman brought me, Right Post, Crossbar and our twins out and stood us up. He woke Crossbar by giving him a bang. Oh, then Mr Net came along and was clipped onto us. Finally, the whistle came. Alisson (our goalkeeper) whacked Mr Bar. Southampton on the attack, Van Dijk slid Ward-Prowse. *Free-kick.* I was anxious about getting hit. Ref's whistle, he stepped up and banged right into the angle of me, it hurt loads! Anyway, Mr Crossbar *cried!* I mean, such a baby. Anyway, Super Sam is about to take a penalty, so *bye, aah...!*

Monty Priest (10)
Yarlet School, Yarlet

The Life Of A Pen

Dear Diary,

Today, it was an early start. I woke up at 5:30am; it was hard, let me tell you. Anyway, I got to work writing and I had a big exam today. I didn't know if I could make it. It was fine though, I had a full ink, but Jeffery had been put in the bin.

My lid has been put back on and I am taking a break for some lunch. If you were wondering what my name is, it's Bob. Just checked my ink and it's half full, still good.

Okay, I am going back to the paper now. Not much left to write now, only 300 more words left, hopefully, I can do it.

So close to finishing; 100 more left.

Oh no! I don't have lots of ink left. *No!* I am out... but I did it! Wait, he's putting me in the bin. Please, no! But I did it. Why?!

Boom! Tink! Just like that, I am in the bin. Goodbye...

Alexander McClean (10)
Yarlet School, Yarlet

The Slay Pig

Dear Diary,

Today, I painted my nails red, white and green. I bought a new wig from Wig Pig as well, the wig has long hair which is green. But the best thing about today was I got the brightest pink lipstick, like wow! I got the most slay fake eyelashes on the whole entire farm, all the other non-slay animals were *so* jealous. But the person who was the most jealous was the farmer, he was so jealous that he threw me out of the farm, onto the road. The big machine made of metal didn't like my slayness; that thing was *so* sassy. The humans inside didn't like my slayness either, they just started screaming *loud*, like really loud. So, I had a headache and I got *mad*, so I stormed and charged at the machine and *bang!* Oh, that's not slay. *Slay, sisters!*

Dillan Siddiqi (11)
Yarlet School, Yarlet

The Boy Who Fell In Love

Dear Diary,

Today, I found my one and only true love. Her eyes are like shiny blue diamonds and her hair is silky soft. I love her, I just hope she loves me back. I met her at a purple lake under a big willow tree. She stared deep into my eyes and I stared deep into her eyes. I feel like we have a real connection together but, suddenly, out of nowhere, a bird flew in-between us. I was so angry at what that bird did, I really thought we were going to kiss under that beautiful tree.

The next day, I asked if she wanted to have a picnic and she said yes. I knew this was my shot. So, we met up and I said, "I like you, I really do," and I kissed her. My heart pumped. Then, out of nowhere, she kissed me back.

And, since then, we have been together.

Harriet Moffatt (10) & Annabel
Yarlet School, Yarlet

SpongeBob's Worst Day Ever

Dear Diary,

I am SpongeBob and I was going to my job, but first I fed my snail. Bye, snail.

At work, I found a wand. I wondered what it does; will it give me food? No. What about a pencil? No. What next? Maybe a picture of James Bond? *Noooo.* What does this cheesenick do? Oh no, I said a bad word. I was going to the moon. I was so sad, "Please help me, Mr. Krabs!"

Mr. Krabs said, "Sorry, I am working."

Okay, let's try it again. "Slipry, slap, slipry, show a wish for a dancing, rainbow cheeseburger." Yes, it worked! Yes, yes, yes, free cheeseburgers for everyone!

"I love you."

"I love you."

Thank you, world, this was the *best* day ever. *Whooooo...*

Emma Wells (10)

Yarlet School, Yarlet

My Experience At Alton Towers

Dear Diary,

Today, I went to Alton Towers with my brother, sister and my dad, and it was really fun! Except for one ride...

Everything was fine until we walked past the scariest ride of all... 'The Smiler'. 'The Smiler'; what type of name is that? More like 'The Terrifying'. My family loves The Smiler, so my family has always wanted me to try it but I was terrified of going on it. Suddenly, my dad started telling me, "You know, if you go on it I will buy you that Fitbit..."

Megan McNulty (11)
Yarlet School, Yarlet

Sassy Cat

Dear Diary,

I am Luna, a kind, caring cat. Now I need some food, so I should go upstairs and claw my humans to get them up. Come on, I need food, *miaow, miaow, miaow!* Hurry up, I don't have all day, I need to suntan.

Wait, what is this? Not gourmet! Well, at least I can sunbathe.

What? The sun is going behind the clouds, *noo!* Well, at least I can do my business now.

Oh no, there is a cat *in my garden. Attack!* Ya, you better run!

And that's the life of Luna.

Harrison Josephs (10)

Yarlet School, Yarlet

160

Into The Gaming World

Dear Diary,

Today, I woke up and went on my computer games and I teleported inside the game. It looked so cool, but I was set on the hardest difficulty. If I wanted to get out of the game, then I would have to do the level. I clicked 'start', it was parkour. I did the first five jumps, but then I failed. I did not give up, and I tried and tried again until I got to the last jump and did it. I teleported out of the game, it was late at night so I went to bed.

Arthur Ratcliffe (9)
Yarlet School, Yarlet

The Basketball

Dear Diary,
I was playing with my two best friends, well, that used to happen, now they are very annoying, silly, mean and pathetic children! And I got very upset and picked up one of them, a mean, spiteful girl called Florence and threw her in the netball hoop. She got her arm stuck in there and started wriggling. I then kicked the other spiteful girl into the football goal. She was the meanest, she was called Clemmie. But then the principal came...

Martha Aitken (11)
Yarlet School, Yarlet

Wicket Split

Dear Diary,

Today, I got split by Jasprit Bumrah. This is how it happened.

So, I was having a good day. That Bumrah, my worst enemy, was going for a speedy 100-miles-per-hour ball, straight at the middle of me, and it was a bullseye. Everyone was so happy, except for me, I was split right in half! I was crying in agony while everyone else was laughing at me, and then, to top it off, I was thrown a hit. It was the worst day of my life.

Anvay Malhotra (10)
Yarlet School, Yarlet

Young Writers Information

We hope you have enjoyed reading this book – and that you will continue to in the coming years.

If you're the parent or family member of an enthusiastic poet or story writer, do visit our website **www.youngwriters.co.uk/subscribe** and sign up to receive news, competitions, writing challenges and tips, activities and much, much more! There's lots to keep budding writers motivated!

If you would like to order further copies of this book, or any of our other titles, then please give us a call or order via your online account.

Young Writers
Remus House
Coltsfoot Drive
Peterborough
PE2 9BF
(01733) 890066
info@youngwriters.co.uk

Join in the conversation!
Tips, news, giveaways and much more!

f YoungWritersUK   **YoungWritersCW**   **youngwriterscw**

 Scan me to watch The Incredible Diary Of video!